Their first kiss was simple, yet it was powerful. Scott didn't want to scare her off by letting his control slip. Slow, he reminded himself as he lightly touched her lips with his own, gently nibbling on them. It was torture, but he dared not trust himself to touch her in any other way, not yet.

Vanessa was in a state of wonder as Scott kissed her—wondering why she had waited so long to taste his mouth, wondering how lips so firm could feel so soft.

She wanted more. Much more.

FATE

PAMELA LEIGH STARR

Genesis Press, Inc.

Indigo Love Stories

An imprint of Genesis Press, Inc.
Publishing Company

Genesis Press, Inc.
P.O. Box 101
Columbus, MS 39703

ISBN-13: 978-1-58571-258-8
ISBN-10: 1-58571-258-2
Manufactured in the United States of America

First Edition 1999
Second Edition 2007

Visit us at www.genesis-press.com or call at 1-888-Indigo-1

DEDICATION

To Chuck,
my husband...
my capricious assistant...
my soulmate...

To Jos,
my teacher...
my advisor...
my friend...

CHAPTER ONE

Ump! Vanessa Lewis grunted as one child, then another, landed on her stomach. Air rushed out of her lungs. What a wake up call! There's nothing in the world like the feel of two small children using your stomach as a trampoline. Add to that a six-year-old tickling your feet, and you are guaranteed to be wide awake. In a flash, Vanessa retaliated with a tickle attack.

"Auntie Ness! Auntie Ness!" three giggling children yelled. "We give up!" Tony, the oldest, got away while the trampolinists, three- and four-year-old Mark and Jasmine remained trapped in Vanessa's clutches. Vanessa declared herself the winner as she grabbed them for a hug. They all rolled across the living room floor where they held their monthly slumber party. The four of them ate popcorn, drank juice, and watched hour after hour of Disney videotapes. The kids would become mesmerized by the screen until they'd turn into zombies and fall asleep. It was all part of the fun. The challenge of the night was trying to stay up the longest. Jasmine, this time, outlasted them all. Vanessa shook her head in shame. She couldn't hang with a four-year-old. That was pretty bad.

This night had been dubbed "Movie Night with Auntie Ness" by her oldest sister Monica, mother of the trio. Vanessa, twenty-three and single, loved having her niece and nephews over, especially since it gave her widowed sister a break. This new tradition began as a way for her sister to have some time alone after the funeral. Monica had been so grief stricken Vanessa knew she had to do some-

thing to help relieve her sister's pain. So Vanessa, being
Vanessa, used a slumber party to cheer up her niece and
nephews. That first party was the exact opposite of the ones
they enjoyed now. It had ended with lots of tears, hugs, and
comforting. It had been exactly what they needed.

Keith had been a wonderful husband, father and
brother-in-law. He and Monica had been the perfect
example of the perfect couple. Vanessa sighed. It would be
wonderful if she could meet somebody who was that
perfect for her. But she wasn't in a rush. The few men she
was interested in enough to date did nothing for her. Not
that she wanted them to do anything for her. She just didn't
feel anything special when she was with them; no sparks, no
chemistry, nothing. Maybe something was wrong with her.
She didn't know and decided it was best not to dwell on it.

The room had suddenly turned quiet, Vanessa realized,
while she'd been preoccupied wjth thoughts of Monica and
men. Monica and men? No way. After Keith, Monica swore
there would be no one else. But there would be someone—
some man—for her, one day, if the sparks flew. She opened
her eyes a little to see what the kids were doing. They just
sat staring at her. Vanessa quickly closed her eyes again
pretending to sleep, waiting to see what they'd do next.

Tony shook her, then Jasmine, and finally Mark.

"Wake up, Auntie Ness," begged Mark.

"She's not sleeping," Tony told them knowingly.

"How do you know?" Jasmine asked her oldest brother.

"I just know," he said with confidence. "Besides, Auntie
Ness is taking us to a surprise—she wouldn't go back to

sleep when she promised. And she's the one who has to drive."

Unable to hold back a chuckle at this six-year-old-logic, Vanessa got up and dragged all three kids along, two attached to her legs and one with a super grip on her arm. They headed for the bathroom. She let the boys go in first.

As Vanessa waited for them to finish she smiled to herself. Kids and the things they said constantly amazed and amused her. Her constant interaction with children didn't make them any less surprising.

Noticing Jasmine bouncing around, Vanessa saw that she had an emergency on her hands. The culprit, she knew, was that extra juice box Jasmine drank after the boys had fallen asleep.

"Come on, boys, make it quick. We ladies have to use the bathroom, too."

"I'm just making sure Mark rinses his hands. You know how he likes to keep soap on them," explained Tony, coming out of the bathroom. "He thinks he's Bubble Man, Auntie Ness."

Jasmine ran in, and from the sound of it, made it just in time.

Vanessa checked Mark's hands. "No bubbles, good."

"But I like bubbles. How can I be Bubble Man without bubbles, Auntie Ness?" Mark asked.

"You can save it for the bathtub," Vanessa told him.

"Okay, but, Auntie Ness, come here." Standing on tiptoe, he motioned her closer.

Vanessa stooped down to listen.

"What's the surprise?" Mark asked in a loud whisper.

"I can't tell you, Mark. Then it wouldn't be a surprise anymore."

"You can tell Bubble Man," he insisted.

"Okay I'll tell Bubble Man tonight, when you're in the tub," Vanessa agreed.

"All right!" Mark shouted, not realizing that he'd been tricked. As he went into the kitchen Vanessa could hear him brag to Tony, "Auntie Ness is going to tell Bubble Man the secret tonight."

Vanessa knew Mark would be back any second. Tony would let him know he'd been fooled. She knocked on the bathroom door. "Wash your face and brush your teeth while you're in there, Jazz."

Mark came running out of the kitchen. "Auntie Ness you tricked me!"

She grabbed him and tickled his little round stomach. "That'll teach you to try to get secrets out of me!" she told him, swinging him back down. "Now go help Tony get the stuff out for the pancakes. I'll be right there."

Mark ran to do as he was told.

Making pancakes after the slumber party was part of the ritual, but the surprise was an extra treat for the kids as well as Monica.

After finally getting to use the bathroom facilities herself, Vanessa came into the kitchen to find a bowl, a box of pancake mix, and a dozen eggs on the floor with a teary-eyed Mark standing right in the middle of the mess.

"We could make scrambled eggs," Tony suggested.

"I don't think so, they'd be too crunchy," Vanessa joked, holding up a broken eggshell and making light of the situation, hoping to stop Mark's tears before they began to fall.

"I-I-I'm-m sorry," Mark stammered.

"It's okay, Mark."

"Oh no!" Jasmine moaned as she walked into the kitchen. "No pancakes!"

"Of course we'll have pancakes. Let's clean up this mess and then go to the grocery."

Everyone helped, causing the job to take twice as long as necessary. But twenty minutes and a roll of paper towels later, the floor was cleaner than when they started. Unfortunately, they were a mess. Vanessa quickly got the kids washed and helped them to get dressed. She combed Jasmine's hair into two neat pigtails, brushed the boys' hair, and sat them down to watch TV and went to get dressed herself.

Vanessa went into her closet and took out a pair of jeans. As she opened the door she looked at herself in the full-length minor. She thought, *Hey, I look pretty cute today.* Laughing, Vanessa slipped on the jeans that fit snugly and showed off her hips and rear end. Being very tall and energetic saved her from becoming heavy, because she happened to be a big-boned woman—not at all like one of those tiny women that a breeze could blow over. She gave herself another look over, a thoughtful expression on her face. She'd be considered fine by any black man. Hey, she'd be considered fine by any man, black, white, red, or yellow. She laughed to herself, thinking how ridiculous she sounded. She put on a bra and t-shirt, silently thanking

God for not endowing her with huge breasts, like her sister Tracy. Vanessa thought she was the perfect size. Not too big, and not too small. She plopped a jean cap on her head, vowing to hot curl her hair after breakfast. Vanessa then went to get her niece and nephews for the trip to the grocery store.

Old Mother Hubbard couldn't have been any worse off than I am, thought Scott Halloway. A Saturday morning with a cupboard so bare an echo could be heard as he opened the door.

"Daddy, Daddy, Daddy." Scott looked down at his two-year-old daughter Megan and grinned. That "daddy, daddy, daddy" was the same song he heard when he woke up every morning and continued to hear until he put her to bed at night. At times he became exasperated. But he knew he'd miss it if Megan stopped singing the daddy song.

Scott picked up his daughter, gave her a hug, and sat her on the counter as he took one more look into the cupboard. Realizing there was nothing hidden behind a can of asparagus and a giant box of potato flakes, Scott sang the nursery rhyme, Old Mother Hubbard.

When he sang the part about the cupboard being bare, his older daughter, Vicki, joined in. Megan demanded to get down, and the girls swung around while Vicki sang the nursery rhyme. Megan tried her best to sing, making up most of the words on her own.

"Okay, okay," Scott said, "This Old Daddy Hubbard's gonna fill that cupboard, but let's get dressed first."

It was times like this that all the pressure of being a single parent was well worth it. Just seeing his children bouncing around and being plain happy helped Scott get through the daily grind of dressing, feeding, and caring for his daughters all alone. He didn't like to think about it. It made Scott miss his wife too much and reminded him of his negligence to both his wife and daughters. But now Scott was determined to be a good parent. He took the responsibility of raising his daughters seriously.

Glancing at the clock, Scott was shocked to see that the girls had let him sleep a little longer than usual. It would take about an hour to get his two little terrors dressed and ready to go. He was really proud of the time he'd cut from that chore. It used to take a little over two hours.

He planned on getting to the store when it opened at eight o'clock. Scott avoided crowds as much as possible. Then, there would be a smaller chance of losing sight of his very active, very small daughters, who refused to sit in a grocery cart.

Forty-five hair-raising minutes later, after dressing Megan twice, compromising with Vicki on what to wear, unclogging the bathroom sink filled with wet tissue paper, and mopping up a huge puddle left over from Megan's tissue experiment, Scott was ready to walk out the door. He'd even beaten his record by fifteen minutes. To stop any unforeseen disaster on the trip from the house to the car he held one child on each hip. Then the phone rang. Scott started to let it ring, but thought it might be his mother-in-law calling long distance. She regularly checked up on them, and he didn't want her to worry. Because she would. Her initials should have been W.W. for Worry Wart. Scott leaned forward so Vicki could pick up the phone. She held it to his ear, then Scott used his shoulder to keep it there, a familiar routine that Scott and Vicki mastered after having to replace two phones.

"Hello."

"Hello...Scott?" A familiar voice asked.

"I'm here, Wendy." Oh great. Would it be Wendy, the wife-hunting, mother-seeking matchmaker today, or just plain Wendy, his sister? She believed the only way he'd be content was to remarry. The idea had begun to appeal to him because he was starting to get lonely. But he didn't even want to consider the women Wendy picked. They were...there were too many words to describe how unsuitable they were. For someone who had his best interest at heart, Wendy was doing a horrible job at matchmaking.

"Our cupboard's bare!" shouted Vicki into the phone.

Megan joined in with, "Daddy, daddy, daddy Hubbar'!"

"Tell the girls I said hi."

"Aunt Wendy says hi, girls," he told his daughters and without missing a beat asked, "Okay, what's up, Wendy?"

"You don't have to sound so grumpy. Did you just wake up?"

"No, as a matter of fact I was about to walk out the door carrying my two lovely ladies." Scott smiled at his daughters.

"Oh, where are you going this time of morning?"

"Just to the grocery. We've run out of food."

"Oh, now I understand what the girls mean. Okay, I'll make it quick. I just called to see if you'd join me for lunch today. Jack's taking Kyle and Brandon to Storyland and wanted to take the girls, too."

"Storyland, who's going to Storyland?" Scott could hear Jack's voice over the line.

"You are, and you know it," Scott heard Wendy's muffled answer.

Kyle and Brandon were Wendy and Jack's six- and seven-year-old sons.

"Are you sure Jack's going to Storyland?" he asked because he knew how Jack loved to tease her and just for the sake of tormenting her.

"Of course he is. He's just being difficult. He's already told the boys, so he can't get out of it now."

Scott paused, still suspicious. "Who else is going to be there?"

"At Storyland? I have no idea. I'm sure lots of families will be there. This is one of those gorgeous days we get in January sometimes—"

"Who else?" Scott asked again, interrupting her.

"Oh, you meant at lunch," Wendy said innocently. "Why do you ask? Just me of course. I only wanted to spend some time with my little brother."

"I'm supposed to believe that? I don't have the time or the patience for this, Wendy. I'm standing here holding two very small girls, who feel like they weigh a ton." Scott refused to let them go and cause more havoc. "Now, I repeat, who else will be there?"

Wendy hesitated, but a disgusted grunt from Scott made her confess.

"A friend of mine from work might pass by."

"Mm-mmm. Just what I thought. Thanks, but no thanks, Wendy. Your friends are too weird."

"Weird!" Wendy was appalled. "How can you—"

"Bye, Wendy. My arms feel like lead. Say bye, girls."

"Bye, Aunt Wendy!" they shouted.

"Wait, Scott, what store are you going to?"

"Schwegmann, right around the corner. Why?"

"Oh, that's okay. I thought you might be going to the Winn-Dixie. There's a special today. Thanks, I'll let you go, bye."

That was a suspicious turn around, but Scott didn't have time to dwell on it.

"Daddy, Daddy, Daddy! Go potty!" Megan demanded.

And when a two-year-old demands to go potty, Scott had learned, you take her quick.

So much for breaking his record, Scott mused, following Megan into the bathroom.

CHAPTER TWO

Scott released a sigh as he made it to the grocery store and pulled into the lot near a black Ford Explorer. He watched a young woman deftly put three small children into a cart. There was no kicking, screaming, or yelling as the two smaller kids sat in the back, and the older one sat in the front. This made Scott determined to put Vicki and Megan into a cart. If she could handle three kids with no problem, he should have no problem with two.

As the woman started moving, Scott couldn't help but notice that she had a gorgeous figure, from behind at least. A nice round behind and long, long legs. Just then she and the cart turned around. She noticed him right away. And boy, just looking at her face to face, for just a second made him feel...

He tried to find the words and couldn't. That was just it, she made him feel. He had a tingling sensation of excitement all over. He'd never been attracted to a black woman before. And he couldn't even see all of her face with that cap on.

"Daddy, Daddy, Daddy!" shouted Megan inside the car.

"Daddy, why are you looking at that lady?" Vicki asked loud enough for anyone to hear. This brought Scott out of his trance. Still, he couldn't help but watch the woman from the corner of his eye, as she returned to her car. What was she getting? A stuffed rabbit?

Scott felt foolish. This was ridiculous. She'd gone back to get one of her kids' toys. So why was he staring at this woman, a black woman at that, who was probably married and now thinking he was some kind of weirdo. Despite his own warning Scott once again found himself staring, and just in time for her to look straight at him as she slammed the car door.

He spun and quickly took his daughters out of the car, trying to get to the entrance before the woman and avoid further embarrassment. Once he was inside the store Scott felt better and put the encounter down to his libido picking up after over a year of abstinence. Any woman would make him feel that way. Who was he kidding? Wendy had already paraded half a dozen women in front of him, and none of them had made him feel like this.

"Daddy, Daddy, Daddy! Go!"

Megan's insistence to get down reminded Scott of his vow. Grabbing a nearby cart and putting Vicki in the back was surprisingly easy. Megan, on the other hand, voiced her opinion the way all two-year-olds have done for years. There was yelling. And there was screaming. The kicking and the swinging of arms was making it extremely difficult for Scott to keep a grip on her. And she was just warming up. Her face had just turned beet red, her arms and legs seemed to multiply, and Scott was really getting embarrassed.

A distant rattle of spinning wheels caught his attention. It became increasingly louder as he tried to determine the source of the sound. A feeling of danger caused him to jump to the side pushing the basket forward as he somehow gripped Megan in a football hold, legs still kicking. He turned. The woman from the parking lot, the gorgeous woman from the parking lot with a figure to die for, barely missed ramming him from behind. He froze. She froze. And, thank God, Megan froze. His eyes made a slow journey up and down the length of her body. The feeling of danger remained. His heart was beating so fast he was sure it was going to pop right out of his body. He couldn't utter a sound. Scott noticed that her cap had fallen off; he could do nothing but stare. Her eyes were beautiful. Big, brown, beautiful, laughing eyes. She had a clear, smooth complexion that was a bit darker than café au lait, a New Orleans delight he'd discovered when he first moved into town a month ago. Her black hair was a short style that came just below her ears. But it was all over her head after her mad dash through the parking lot. She didn't look old enough to be the mother of three. This was confirmed when Scott heard the little boy in front holding a stopwatch say, "That was ten seconds, Auntie Ness!"

Scott looked at her left hand: no wedding ring. He shook himself. Why should he care? This woman almost hit him with a grocery cart. Almost. Yet he felt as if he'd been knocked over. And as ridiculous as it sounded, all that he could think to say was, "You have an interesting way of handling a grocery cart."

"I'm sorry," Vanessa stammered, realizing that she appeared at worse to be a maniac, or at the very least a very irresponsible person. She tried to hide her embarrassment. "I'm sorry if I scared you. There was really no chance of me hitting you. I'm very experienced with this." She turned away to hide a grin. The expression on his face was hilarious.

This whole cart-racing idea had started out so innocently a year ago. It was simply a matter of getting out of the rain and into the store. The kids got a kick out of Vanessa running across the parking lot and begged their aunt to race every time they went to the store together, and then Tony got a Mickey Mouse stopwatch for his birthday. That was about the time it started to get out of hand. This was bound to happen, Vanessa thought, dreading to face him again.

"What I mean is…"

"Auntie Ness," Tony interrupted. "Did you hear? That was ten seconds, we broke our record! Can you believe it?"

"Yes, Tony, um, that was great."

Tony looked at his aunt as if she'd lost her mind. This was the best they'd done at cart racing.

"What's wrong, Auntie Ness?" asked Jasmine.

"What's a record?" Mark wanted to know.

Vanessa normally loved to answer questions but decided to put them off in light of the situation. "We'll talk about it later," she whispered, hoping that would be the end of the questions.

She looked at the man she had almost hit. "I'm really sorry," she said, trying to keep a straight face. "I'm not crazy, you know. I really am a nice, sane person."

He didn't say anything, just kept staring at her with that strange look on his face. Vanessa wondered what he was thinking but wisely chose not to make any attempts to find out.

"Oh, well, have a nice day. Bye!" She moved away quickly, before the man recovered and decided to lecture her on the importance of setting a good example to children.

As she walked away Vanessa heard that man laughing at her. It was how she began to think of him: that man. She had noticed him right away as he pulled into the parking lot. She got her first glimpse through his open window. And wham! It hit her. She couldn't describe it. It was like some kind of pull. And the thing about it was, he wasn't all that good looking, not knock out, totally irresistibly good-looking. But definitely cute. He was tall, a few inches over six feet, which would certainly be a requirement. He had blond hair, dark blond, and she liked the way it curled across his forehead. She must be crazy! That man was getting a reaction from her she had never experienced before.

He had her staring at him like a love-starved fool, talking like a total nut, and apologizing all over the place. Exactly why was she apologizing anyway? After all, she'd missed hitting him altogether. Lucky for her, she sheepishly admitted to herself.

Besides, he was off limits simply because of all the problems dating a white man would cause. Vanessa knew, because she had friends in an interracial marriage. They seemed happy, but even they admitted to it being hard. And marriage was hard enough these days without any extra pressure. Besides, that man looked good and married, and to a white woman at that.

Vanessa slowly became aware that Jasmine, Tony, and Mark were whispering to each other. "What are you guys talking about?" she asked.

"Oh, nothing," said Jasmine. "It's just that we've passed the eggs three times. We wanted to know if you're still going to buy some?"

"Yeah, are you all right, Auntie Ness?" asked Tony.

Oh my goodness, thought Vanessa, I didn't do that! That man did not cause her to act like that! She headed straight to the dairy section and grabbed a carton of eggs none too gently, then checked to see if any were damaged from her rough handling. Another carton of broken eggs was the last thing they needed. She quickly headed to the checkout area. Vanessa needed to get out of the store before she accidentally bumped into that man again. While paying for her eggs and, surprisingly, nothing else, Vanessa looked down the aisle and saw him talking to some woman. A white woman with long blond hair, just like the little girls, and a slender figure like a model. Probably his wife. And I bet he's telling her all about the crazy lady who almost rammed into him.

He looked up. And to Vanessa's surprise he didn't appear to be too happy with the woman. They'd probably had a fight or something. But then he spotted her, smiled, and waved. Vanessa gave him a naval salute and fled, pushing the cart in front of her.

While walking down the one aisle all children can't resist, Scott was attacked. It was what he referred to as a Wendy attack. His wonderful sister, the eternal match-maker, had set him up. That was why she wanted to know what store he was going to. She must have called her friend…what did she say her name was?…Bee-Bee, Cee-Cee, Dee-Dee. Something like that. He didn't know. But it ended with a double-e. She made sure he knew that for some reason. Wendy must have sent her to 'accidentally' bump into him at the grocery store. She must be desperate, Scott thought, watching the woman with the double-e at the end of her name try to humor his daughters by talking about cereal.

It was then that he spotted the lady with the beautiful eyes at the checkout. The children had called her Auntie Ness. The name fit; it was different. She was different. Different from the other women he had the misfortune of meeting, via his sister, of course. And none of them did for him what this woman had done. Ness had made him laugh at himself again. He had been far too serious for far too long. Scott had laughed so hard that his children had stared at him in amazement. Grocery clerks and a bagger looked at him curiously, but it hadn't bothered him. It felt good to let loose. It was a hilarious situation, and a pleasant one too, because Ness was one good looking woman. Ness had curves, and plenty of them. Nothing like this double-e woman who was all skinny and pointy. Mentally comparing them, Scott frowned at the double-e woman. Scott caught Ness staring at him, so he smiled and waved. She saluted, and walked out the door with the pride of a queen.

Scott chuckled. His laughter caught the double-e woman's attention. She was openly devouring him with her eyes. It gave him the creeps.

"Daddy's been laughing a lot today!" That came from Vicki.

"Oh, I hope that means your daddy is in a good mood. If he is, maybe we could spend some time together," she said, eyeing him again.

There was no mistaking the invitation in her eyes. She was trying to pick him up. And right in front of his daughters. Again, Scott wondered what Wendy could possibly be thinking when she chose these women.

"I don't think so—um, what was your name?" asked Scott again.

"Dee-Dee with a double-e." she answered.

"Oh yeah, Dee-Dee," he paused, "with a double-e. I have a lot to do today, thanks."

"Sure, if you say so. You have some nice kids. I'll say goodbye to them." As Dee-Dee leaned over the cart to say goodbye Vicki said in a loud whisper, "Daddy's been laughin' a lot because of the brown lady. She almost hit him with a cart."

"Oh," said Dee-Dee. "A brown lady?"

"Brown, brown, brown," added Megan.

Scott grabbed the grocery cart and quickly moved away from Dee-Dee. He didn't want to explain or share anything about his encounter with Ness.

"Nice meeting you, Bee-Bee," he lied.

"That's Dee-Dee, with a double-e," she reminded him.

Funny how he could remember Ness's name after hearing it only once. "Oh, okay, Dee-Dee, bye." And good riddance.

CHAPTER THREE

Storyland or Audubon Zoo, those were Vanessa's choices. After comparing the expenses involved, her teacher's salary demanded that Storyland be the surprise. Everyone raced to the entrance with Mark beating them there. The winner pushed the button at the entrance to Storyland. Since Mark had never had a turn before, he became the winner by silent agreement. They listened to a statue of the Cheshire Cat from Alice in Wonderland greet them, then went to pay the admission fee.

Storyland was definitely built with children in mind, thought Vanessa as she bent down to enter the park grounds. The entrance past the ticket window was about four feet high. It was sure to make children feel welcome, but to adults it was pretty uncomfortable. At least for adults over five feet tall.

They were just in time for the puppet show being announced throughout the park. Tony grabbed Mark's hand, and Jasmine pulled Vanessa along. They ran past Captain Hook's pirate ship and across a small wooden bridge to the puppet castle. They got great seats right in front. There were rows of small wooden and plastic benches waiting for kids to come and enjoy the show. There were even a few large benches along the back for big kids like Vanessa. Mark and Tony sat in one, and Jasmine sat next to them on another bench. Vanessa sat on the ground beside them.

"Auntie Ness, what's the name of the puppet show?" asked Jasmine.

"I don't know, Tony," Vanessa instructed. "Go read the sign on the outside of the puppet theater."

Tony was a first grader and an excellent reader already. He loved to show off his skills as often as possible. Tony came back and proudly announced, "It's called, 'Who's in Rabbit's House?' "

"Oh, I know that story, we heard it in school," said Jasmine. "It was good."

"And I'm sure it will be again," answered Vanessa.

Soon the benches were filled. The ground, too, became crowded with little people anxious for the show to start. To give them more room Vanessa graciously gave up her seat, sitting instead on the adult benches behind, but still within sight of the children.

Just as the show began, Vanessa's view was blocked by a very firm and very nice-looking behind. Then she heard a small voice say, "Daddy, Daddy, Daddy."

Without even looking up to see his face she knew it was that man. He sat his little girls in the last row of wooden benches directly in front of her. He got them settled, and quickly moved, depriving Vanessa of a fantastic view. It was a great view, but she was relieved when he left. How that man made her nervous, and shaky—and sweaty? she thought, wiping her palms on her jeans.

Trying to pull herself together, Vanessa began talking to herself, not a good idea, but at the moment she needed to talk to someone. Thank God, he didn't see me. But where did he go? I can't believe he'd leave these little girls here all alone. Out of the corner of her eye Vanessa could see him standing on the sidelines watching his daughters. I just hope he doesn't spot me. And stop talking to yourself, she admonished.

Vanessa tried to concentrate on the puppet show. She watched her niece and nephews participate with the rest of the audience. Clapping, foot stomping, and sawing were a few of the motions the children were enthusiastically participating in. Mark peered at Vanessa over his little shoulder expectantly, so what could she do but participate? Besides, this was the fun part. Vanessa had been here often for birthday parties and visits with her other nieces and nephews. She enjoyed the shows so much and laughed so loud the performers knew her by name.

Vanessa felt like a big kid herself. Not only did she participate, but did it with so much enthusiasm that she felt as if she was a part of the cast itself, that she belonged here surrounded by storybook characters and children. She felt right at home. The excitement and joy she was getting from this one little puppet show was enough to make her happy. She supposed that was one of the reasons she hadn't found anyone she could be interested in. They were all too serious and had goals that never coincided with hers. Unintentionally her thoughts drifted to that man again. She wondered if his goals were the same as hers, a simple enjoyment of life, family, children.

Suddenly, he was standing right in front of her, almost as if she'd summoned him with her thoughts. Then she remembered the little girls were sitting in front of her. He quickly scooped up the smallest one, who Vanessa realized had been making quite a bit of noise. Her eyes followed him as he went to stand on the sidelines. Trying to figure

out the attraction, she couldn't help but take a few, quick
peeks every couple of seconds. When he looked in her
direction again, she glanced down deciding that she needed
to retie a perfectly tied shoelace. Vanessa knew she should
be ashamed of herself, using one of her students' ploys to
avoid staying out of trouble. And that man was trouble.

Forcing herself to watch the show and not him,
Vanessa's attention was immediately brought back to him.
The little girl he'd been holding was giving him a hard time.
He was having trouble holding onto her. She was
squirming to get down and yelling. With a look full of frustrated patience that man came right back toward her,
squirming child and all. Vanessa thought he was going to
drop the child into her lap because of the purposeful
expression on his face. Instead he gently put her back into
her place. She was immediately quiet. But he didn't move.
He stood right in front of her. His eyes focused directly on
her. She began to wonder if she had bits of pancake on her
face from this morning's breakfast. She could tell he wanted
to say something. Vanessa wanted him to say something.
And he did.

"Hello, again," he whispered, then walked away.

Hello again, sweet and simple, in a deep voice that sent
chills down her spine. That was nice, too nice. The steady
sound of loud clapping made Vanessa aware that the show
was over. She quickly gathered her niece and nephews to
play in the park. Her plan was to avoid him.

Vanessa knew from experience that keeping an eye on
three small, active children in Storyland was a huge task.
They ran from the spider's web, to Little Miss Muffet's, to

the slide coming down Jack and Jill's hill. Then they ran to the fire truck, the mermaid pond, and back to the spider's web again. While keeping track of her little gang, Vanessa saw that man and his kids all over the park. The poor man couldn't keep up with them. At one point, he was carrying one who was demanding to get down while the other one ran to get inside a giant whale, nearly falling into the water surrounding it. It was comical, but Vanessa felt sorry for him, too.

On one occasion she saw him talking to someone. The girls seemed to be giving him a break because they were both in the fire truck. Vanessa heard him say, "Yeah, Wendy set me up." That voice, her spine responded again with a shiver. She wanted to stay just to listen to him, but she kept going. Who was Wendy, she wondered. His wife?

Having tired of running all around the park, Vanessa suggested face painting.

"All right!" yelled Tony.

"I want a snake!" requested Mark.

"Yeah, and I want a flower on each side," said Jasmine, pointing to both her cheeks.

"Sounds good to me," agreed Vanessa. Standing in line gave her a much-needed break. They looked at the different pictures they could choose from and discussed what colors to use. The face painting was near the Mermaid Pond. There was a sign that said 'NO CLIMBING ON THE ROCKS' in big bold letters. And it never failed to irritate Vanessa when parents allowed their children to do just that. From the corner of her eye she spotted a little girl climbing on the rocks. Vanessa looked around for a parent before advising her to get down. Then she noticed another little one bouncing up and down near the pond. She was shouting "Vicki! Vicki! Vicki! Up, up, up!"

Before she could spot anyone, the little girl slipped, fell, and hit the back of her head on the ground. Thank goodness it wasn't cement but grass she'd landed on.

Vanessa's first reaction was to comfort the little girl, but someone got there before her, asking where her mommie was.

That's when she realized it was that man's little girls. Vanessa looked around but didn't see him anywhere. Meanwhile one of the face painters scooped the child up and carried her to the park office. She'd also grabbed the hand of Vicki's little sister. They were both crying their eyes out. Where was their dad? He probably didn't have any idea where they were.

Vanessa pried Tony, Jasmine, and Mark way from the face painting line so she could find that man to tell him about his little girls. She found him still standing near the fire truck calling, "Vicki, Megan, I give up. Daddy's tired of playing hide and seek."

He was looking around, obviously searching for his missing daughters. He thought they were playing hide-and-seek and had no idea that his children had changed the rules to run-and-find.

Vanessa walked up to him. "Your little girl fell. She's in the front office."

He didn't say a word, his face said it all. It changed from slight worry to panic in a matter of seconds. "Which way?"

Vanessa pointed in the direction of the park office. He raced off without another word.

Back in line, Vanessa heard the announcement, "Will Scott Halloway please come to the Storyland office."

So, his name was Scott, thought Vanessa. I like that. Short and sweet, just like his...

"Hello, again." He looked like a Scott. She started to feel guilty about the way she had told him about the accident. Maybe she had been too blunt. She hadn't tried to reassure him or let him know that Vicki didn't seem seriously hurt. But as she stood waiting in line Vanessa began to get a little upset about the whole situation and decided he needed a good scare. If he couldn't handle watching both girls, he shouldn't bring them out by himself. Somebody could have walked away with them without Scott even knowing what happened.

And now she was calling him Scott.

She noticed Tony, the last in line, getting his face painted.

They wouldn't be here too much longer. Then she could get Scott completely out of her mind.

Just as that thought occurred, she spotted him and his girls crossing the small wooden bridge near Captain Hook's pirate ship. Vicki seemed to be fine, but you'd think that after such an incident he'd have gone home. Vanessa thought about telling him exactly that. It looked as if she was going to get her chance because they were walking directly toward her. He stopped right in front of her. Her heart was pounding, and her palms were like a dripping faucet.

"Thank you," Scott said. "I appreciate you coming to find me. I've been trying to get up the nerve to speak to you all morning."

Ignoring that last revealing statement and being grateful that he didn't attempt to shake her hand, Vanessa took a deep breath to steady herself. "It was nothing. But are you sure she's okay? I mean she had a nasty fall. Maybe you should take her home now."

"Vicki's fine. She doesn't have a mark on her. And besides kids tend to bounce back pretty quickly. And Megan here," he pointed his head in her direction, "was only worried about her sister."

Vanessa should have left it at that, especially since that smile of his brought back those nervous, shaky feelings again, but still, it didn't stop her from blurting out, "Maybe you should be a little more worried."

Eyebrows raised, he asked, "You think so?"

That should have been enough of a warning, a subtle one, but definitely a warning. Ness ignored it. "Yes, I do. And next time around, you ought to think about getting a little help."

"So I need help?" he grunted.

"It's just that you seem to have so much trouble keeping up with them," Vanessa answered, thinking she'd gone way too far. He didn't seem to be taking this advice too well.

"I see you don't have the same problem," he replied.

"No, I have a lot of experience. I'm a teacher," she said proudly, as if that explained it all. "You must realize that someone could have walked away with both of your daughters without anyone even noticing."

"So, you're offering me some professional advice, nothing personal?"

"I guess I am," Ness answered, worried by the storm she saw brewing in his eyes. She didn't know this man, just how he made her feel.

"Oh, well then, thanks again. It would have been nice to talk, on a more personal level, that is."

"Good-bye," she choked out, turning away from him. "Come on, kids," Vanessa called, guiding them toward the face house. It was what she called it. The house had many faces, with windows and doors taking the place of eyes, noses and mouths. One particular face showed exactly how she felt. It was the face depicting surprise. Or should she say astonishment? Vanessa had never spoken that way to anyone before, let alone a stranger. And never had she butted into someone else's business, except family, of course. For some reason she just couldn't help it.

Vanessa sat on a bench to watch the children run in and out of the house.

"Five minutes," she called out to them.

She spent that five minutes, which turned into ten, then fifteen, being appalled at her behaviot

"Time to go!" she called finally, shaking herself.

"Okay, Auntie Ness," said Mark, bounding out of a mouth. Jasmine and Tony came running along behind him.

Scott was at the mermaid pond, unsuccessfully fishing. He'd just missed catching one of the little plastic fishies, as

Megan called them. The magnet on the end of the rod just wouldn't connect with the little metal thingy on the fish. He missed again, but this time it was because he was watching her. He was amazed at how quickly Ness's nieces and nephews complied. How did she do it? He knew when it came time to go, his daughters would put up a fight.

Scott admitted that he was a bit upset by her comments, but they were true. He couldn't handle his daughters, and probably wouldn't have come at all if he wasn't trying to stay away from Wendy. After this morning, there was no telling what she'd be up to. Since he had known Jack would be here, Scott had decided to try it out. Too bad Jack had left just when he needed him.

His thoughts switched to Vicki. Scott realized just how lucky she was. If she had landed anywhere but the grass they would be at the hospital right now getting stitches, or having a cast put on her arm or leg, or both. She didn't even have a mark on the back of her head.

He had wanted to leave, but Vicki asked to have her face painted. How could he refuse? Then Megan wanted to go to the mermaid pond…and still, here they were.

He suddenly came up with a perfect solution to his problem. A trip to Burger King would definitely get the girls out of Storyland. "Who's hungry?" Scott asked.

"I am!" answered Vicki.

"Me, me, me!" Megan chimed in.

"Well, let's go to Burger King!" Scott suggested.

"Yeah!" they screeched as they ran to the exit.

Grinning, Scott tapped Anansi the spider's hat at the exit. "I'm almost as tricky as you, Mr. Spider," he told the statue on the way out. Now to find a Burger King that didn't have a playground.

CHAPTER FOUR

Turning down an unfamiliar street and hoping not to get lost, Scott remembered there was a Burger King that catered to college students near the park. Wendy had taken them there when they first moved to New Orleans. It didn't have a playground to tempt little kids and give parents the will-we-ever-get-out-of-here blues.

It seemed that Ness had the same idea because there she was sitting in a booth near the back of the restaurant. She and the three kids were just talking away; they looked like they were enjoying themselves. God, she was beautiful. He just stopped to feel the attraction between them. Scott had never believed in fate before, but in a matter of five hours he'd encountered the same woman three times—and each time was unforgettable. Maybe someone up there was trying to tell him something. Scott decided to listen and this time do something about it.

He stood in line with two surprisingly quiet girls. He got his order and looked around for somewhere to sit. He wanted to be near her, but not too close. He had to choose the perfect position. Scott didn't want to appear pushy. He was definitely interested in getting to know her. She didn't seem to notice him, but it was possible that she was purposely ignoring him. So subtlety was best, but some-times the best-laid plans went haywire, especially with kids around.

Vicki suddenly perked up and yelled, "Daddy, it's the brown lady!" She ran over to Ness and sat at the table next to her booth. What else could Scott do but sit down.

Surprised, Vanessa smiled. "Hi, Vicki, I see you're okay."

"Yeah, and no bumps. Hey, how'd you know my name?" asked Vicki.

"Just magic, I guess."

Vicki's little mouth formed the shape of an O as she slowly shook her head up and down.

"Hello again, I hope she didn't offend you," Scott said as he sat at the table.

"Not at all," answered Vanessa. "Besides," she told Vicki, "I really am purple. Ever heard of the purple people eater?"

"No," Vicki answered wide-eyed.

Vanessa was finding it quite easy to talk to Vicki. So she continued the conversation, prolonging it in an attempt to avoid having to speak to her father.

"Well, that's me. I really am purple. Let me just peel..." Vanessa tried to peel the skin off her hand. By this time she had all the kids' attention, especially Tony's, Jasmine's, and Mark's, who knew very well that their aunt was brown. But she'd been acting pretty weird lately, so they decided to wait and see.

"Oh, no!" Vanessa stared at her hand in mock horror. "I'm not purple! I guess I'm not a purple people eater. I'm just a brown hamburger eater."

All the children laughed.

"So I've noticed," Scott answered.

"Excuse me?" Vanessa asked, knowing her ploy wouldn't work. She couldn't sit here talking to the kids and ignore him.

"I've noticed, that you eat hamburgers and that you're brown," he said with an appreciative look staring at her eyes, moving to and pausing at her breasts maybe a bit longer than he should have. He moved his gaze up again to admire her face with a smooth complexion and unforgettable direct eyes—eyes that were directing him to watch out, or else.

Scott cleared his throat. "We seem to keep bumping into each other."

"Yes, it does seem that way," Vanessa answered.

"Hey, Mister!" Tony shouted, getting everyone's attention, including the people ordering lunch, the restaurant workers, and probably everyone out in the parking lot. "You don't have to worry about getting hit with a cart. Auntie Ness said we're through with cart racing."

Vanessa could feel her ears burn from the blush that seemed to spread all over her face. She'd just finished explaining to Tony, Jasmine, and Mark about the dangers of cart racing. That was when she spotted Scott and his girls. She had pretended not to see them and went on talking to the kids about every and anything. Vanessa had known exactly when he noticed her, and precisely how long he stood and stared. She still had goose bumps from that stare. Then he was so bold as to look her over. He must have memorized the shape of her breasts because he concentrated on them a full minute at least. Maybe that explained why her bra suddenly felt so confining. Funny, it had never bothered her before.

Scott was smiling. "It's nice to know it's safe to go to the grocery again."

If anything, Vanessa's ears got even hotter. "I really am sorry about that. It has never happened before."

"It's perfectly okay. No harm was done, and it's given me a chance to meet a very interesting person. My name's Scott," he said over Vicki's head.

"And I'm Vanessa."

"I wondered what Ness stood for. I heard the kids call you Auntie Ness." He smiled again. "Vanessa's a beautiful name."

"Thanks." Vanessa really didn't know how to respond to this. Was he trying to flirt with her? Wait a minute, she thought. Wasn't this man married? She didn't see a ring, but that didn't mean a thing.

She suddenly realized how quiet the children were. Five pairs of very curious eyes were focused on the two adults. Vanessa needed to do something. She began picking up dirty napkins and hamburger wrappers. "I'm sure your wife has a beautiful name, too."

"Yes, her name was Kathy."

"She's in heaven," added Vicki.

That made Vanessa stop mid-wipe. She paused to stare at a glob of ketchup on the table. Then who was the woman in the store, she wondered as she wiped up the ketchup. "I'm sorry," she said, turning to face Scott again.

"It's been awhile." He couldn't figure out what to say next and realized that he sounded like someone from an old movie. He watched her empty the trays and begin to usher the children toward the door.

The little girl stopped to talk to his daughters. "Hi, I'm Jasmine. What's your name, and your name?"

"I'm Vicki, and that's Megan," Vicki answered.

"Megan-Vicki, Megan-Vicki, Megan-Vicki," sang Megan.

Thankful for the delay, Scott got up and awkwardly stood next to Vanessa. It was now or never.

"Look, since I first saw you in the parking lot, I've been attracted to you. I would like to get to know you."

Her eyes showed surprise and caution. "I don't think so."

Direct, not corny, he coached himself. "Please, think about it. Don't you find it odd for us to have seen each other so often today? Doesn't it seem strange that we keep running into each other? I know this is going to sound like a pick-up line but I was thinking that...maybe...we were destined to meet."

"It does sound like a pick-up line." She smiled. "And, yes, I've noticed," she answered, then surprised him by saying, "I thought you were following me."

When he didn't answer right away she asked, "Were you?"

"What if I said I was?" he asked.

"Then I'd say you were one desperate man."

"I can say the same about you. Were you following me?" he asked right back.

"No, I'm not a desperate woman. A little reckless with shopping carts, but not desperate."

"That doesn't explain why you're so reluctant to talk to me. Tell me why."

"There are lots of reasons I could name."

"Is it because I'm white?"

"Straightforward, aren't you?"

"When I have to be. You don't like white guys?"

"I don't like the problems that come with seeing a white guy. But for some reason, I am attracted to you, and I've been trying to figure out why."

She stood, staring at him as if that was what she was trying to do at this precise moment. Scott just waited, letting her take in her fill as his own eyes did the same. Having her stare at him with such honest appreciation did a lot for his male ego. He'd stand here all day if Nessa wanted to stare. Nessa. He liked it. He repeated it again inside his head as he continued to watch her watching him. That name felt right. It wasn't the one she'd given him, and not what the kids called her, but in his mind fit her even more perfectly than the others.

Encouraged by her interest and her words Scott asked, "Is it necessary to try to figure it out?"

"Definitely. You see, I've never been attracted to a white guy before, and I don't know if I really want to..." She looked straight into his eyes. She didn't notice what color or shape they were. She could concentrate only on their intensity. Oh boy, was that look intense. It made her want—him. For someone who was a novice when it came to flirting, she was doing a whole lot better than she would have thought.

"Are you saying that you don't want to try to figure out this mutual attraction?" asked Scott.

"That's right," she answered, nervously breaking eye contact. "Since that's the case, I'd better be going." With that Vanessa walked away. "Come on kids, it's time to go." And of course they came immediately, ready to follow her out the door. There was no whining, no pleading. She made it all seem so easy.

Scott stood stunned for a few seconds. She liked him, she found him attractive, and she was walking away.

"Nessa, wait!" he called.

She stopped, turned, and looked at him with those expressive brown eyes. "Nessa, I like that, no one calls me Nessa. If it's meant to be, if we really were destined to meet, I'll see you again I'm sure."

Vanessa walked out of the restaurant hoping to never see him again. She couldn't handle that kind of relationship and was glad to have been able to fight the temptation.

Or was she sorry?

CHAPTER FIVE

"Mommie! Mama! Hey M-a-a-a-a!" were the sounds that greeted Monica when Vanessa pulled into the driveway. Three whirlwinds came bounding out of the car to greet their mother. Monica was taking advantage of the warm day to work on her front lawn.

"Oh, I missed you rascals. You were gone almost all day. I think Auntie Ness was trying to keep you all to herself."

"Just trying to give you some extra time after the party, sis."

"I told you it wasn't necessary, Ness, but thanks." Monica appreciated her sister's concern. This was her first outing since Keith's death. It was a birthday party for a friend of hers at work. She knew it was good for her to get out once in awhile, but she missed her children. They were all she had left of Keith.

"So, guys, what was the surprise?" Monica asked.

"We went to Storyland, and I pressed the button," said Mark.

"And we saw a puppet show; it was good," said Jasmine. "A lot better than the story at school. I think they added some parts, it was funny."

"And we went to Burger King," Mark added, trying to top his sister.

"Sounds like you guys had a ball." Monica hugged each of her children.

"We did, and everywhere we went there was this man and his little girls," Tony began.

"Their names were Vicki and Megan," said Jasmine. "And their mommie's in heaven, just like Daddy."

"And they're white!" Mark blurted out.

Glancing at Vanessa, expecting to share a laugh, Monica was surprised to see her sister frowning. She started to ask Nessa what was wrong but was interrupted by Tony adding more news.

"Yeah, and we almost hit him with a grocery cart. The man laughed and laughed at Auntie Ness. I don't think she liked that," Tony whispered to his mom. "That's why we can't do anymore cart racing. But we beat our record, ten seconds, Mom!" he ended with a shout.

As Monica listened to her children recount their day, she watched her youngest sister. Vanessa, of all people, seemed embarrassed. Monica was expecting her to laugh and add a comment like she normally did when the kids shared their adventures. But she was strangely quiet. Something was wrong. Monica sent the kids to play in the backyard with a promise to make cookies later. Vanessa hadn't even realized they were gone. She just sat there, daydreaming. Ness daydreaming!

"Okay girl, what's up? "asked Monica.

Vanessa jumped. "Oh, nothing. Tell me, how was the party? Were there any cute guys? Did you stay long? Did you dance?"

"Ness, I didn't notice any guys. I only stayed till ten, and yes, I danced, with myself, and my friends."

"Ten? The party was probably just getting started. But you did dance? Good!" Vanessa almost shouted. "I was hoping you wouldn't just sit on the sidelines. What dances did you do?" Vanessa chattered. Before Monica could say anything Nessa said, "I know, none of that kiddie stuff. I've seen some pretty wild dances, and they are not for you. I know your style. Since you didn't dance with any guys, and that doesn't surprise me, I'd say you did the Electric Slide, or the old reliable Bus Stop!" Vanessa said as she got up to demonstrate.

Oh yeah, there was a whole lot more going on than she thought, Monica realized. Ness was purposely trying to change the subject with all this talk about the party and dancing. Ness was never that interested in parties. Monica could count with a closed fist the number of parties Ness had gone to in the past year.

"Okay, Ness, enough about the dance. What I want to know is what's up with you? One minute you're staring into space, then talking a mile a minute the next. I mean I should be asking you questions. Did you really hit someone with a grocery cart? And who did you go to Burger King with?"

"Oh, Monica, I didn't want to talk about it, but since the Jones children have already broadcast it, yes, I met a guy. A cute white guy with two kids."

"You met a white guy? And you thought he was cute?"

"Too cute. This whole day was so strange, Monica."

"Strange? I'd say you've got that right. I'm still trying to get over you using 'cute' and 'guy' in the same sentence."

"You're exaggerating, I've never been that picky."

"You haven't?"

"I haven't," Ness insisted.

"So there was nothing wrong with, Derrick, Joseph, and what's his name—?"

"That last one? D'wayne. They were all too self-centered to be cute."

"I understand."

"Monica, how can you understand? I haven't told you anything yet!"

"So tell me," Monica insisted, guiding her sister to have a seat at the kitchen table.

"Wherever I was, wherever I went, he was there. The grocery store, Storyland, Burger King. It was almost as if he was following me. I even accused him of it."

"Oh, Ness," Monica told her, surprised by what her little sister was revealing.

"What?"

"That happy look on your face, that dreamy expression that you're wearing…"

"I'm always happy," Ness answered, brushing aside her sister's speculation.

"But you've never had a look like that on your face when talking about a man. You normally look as if you'd eaten a dead crawfish."

"They're all dead when you eat them."

"You know what I mean, the ones that die before you cook 'em. Which is a perfect analogy. Most men are dead to you before they can even try to get close to you. This guy must be a live one."

"Why are we talking about crawfish? I was talking about Scott."

"Scott, huh? Well go on. If I'm going to help I'm going to need to know everything."

Vanessa slowly shook her head and continued, "Like I was saying before, it was strange. I could almost feel was as if someone or something was trying to get us together. The minute I spotted him in the parking lot it was as if a giant magnet was pulling me straight to him. I resisted, ignored it, but then I almost hit him with a grocery cart. Talk about embarrassing," Vanessa muttered with a self-deprecating laugh as she put her face in her hands.

"Ness, don't feel so bad. You could always blame it on that giant magnet you were talking about. Those grocery carts are metal."

"And Scott was the magnet," she laughed.

"That's a good way of looking at it." Monica's own laughter interrupted her comments—comments that were supposed to make Ness feel better. "You were supposed to hit him. How else were you going to meet him? Otherwise, you would have probably walked right past him. This way you both had an unforgettable first encounter."

"A first encounter of the forgettable kind might have been better."

"Might have?" Monica asked, catching the word that was rarely in Ness's vocabulary in reference to men in general.

"He was cute, Monica."

"There you go with the cute thing again."

Ignoring that last comment Ness told her sister, "I should have listened when mama told me that cart racing was dangerous." Ness sighed and got up to get a glass of water from Monica's cooler. She took a sip of the cold water and sat down on one of the tall brown kitchen stools with that dreamy expression on her face again.

When it looked like she wasn't going to go on, Monica called, "Ness!" Turning serious now, Monica asked, "Is there anything else you need to tell me, Ness? It's hard to believe, but I think I'm witnessing my little sister actually falling for a guy."

"Yeah," she agreed, "but I insulted him."

"You did? Why?" Monica asked.

An indignant look crossed her face. "He'd lost his kids in Storyland. Any pervert could have walked off—with both of them."

"Ness, I know how protective you are about kids, but not enough to go around insulting strangers. If you took the time to do that I know you feel something for him."

"Of course I do. That's why I couldn't help myself. I ogled him."

"Ogled him?" Monica shook her head not really surprised at the term Ness used. She had a tendency to use some weird words sometimes.

"Go on."

"We talked a little in Burger King. That's when I stared holes into him. And I admit, I like him, a lot." She paused and repeated. "A whole lot. And you know there haven't been too many guys who've caught my interest."

What an understatement, Monica thought. Ness had asked Keith to take her to her senior prom, something she and Monica still joked about. Monica was sure that any number of guys would have been dying to take her—Ness simply didn't want to have anything to do with any of them. She'd taken their cousin Daniel, Monica remembered. Not much had changed in the six years since that prom night incident. The three guys she'd mention earlier were the only names she could remember.

"Now," Ness continued, forcing Monica to concentrate on the here and now. "I finally meet one I do feel something for, and he's white. He's got blond hair, of all things. You can't get any whiter than that!"

Monica took a long, hard look at her sister. "So what! I've never seen you like this before, Ness. There's no doubt in my mind that something special's happened to you. I don't know, maybe it's because I've just lost the love of my life, but I think you should give this guy a chance."

"But Monica—"

"Don't think about him being black or white. Think about him being right or wrong for you. I never told you, but when Keith and I first met, the attraction was unbelievable. It was so strong, nothing could keep us apart. And if you feel something like that for somebody, then you'd better not take a chance on not knowing for sure. Take it from me, life's too short for that."

"Oh, I know, Monica. Keith was unique, wonderful, but what's the use? Scott tried to talk to me, and I walked away. I told him if it was meant to be we'd meet again. I'll probably never see him again."

"Who knows, Ness. You just might."

"You know, he asked if I didn't like white guys. I guess he thought I was prejudiced because I kept ignoring him. I couldn't help but think about Jessica and Adam, and the problems they've got to deal with." Jessica and Adam were family friends. They'd known Jessica long before Adam, and if anyone would have told Jessica eight years ago that she'd be married to a white man, she would have called them a liar.

"I understand what you're saying, but Jessica and Adam don't have problems with each other. It's other people that they have problems with. Think about it."

Ness smiled, "That's what he told me, to think about it." She hugged her sister. "I'll see you later. Tell the kids bye for me."

Before Monica could stop her, Vanessa hopped in her Ford Explorer and took a drive to the lake. She parked and walked up to the levee, a small man-made, grassy hill used to protect the city from floodwaters.

Sitting at the top, Vanessa had a good view of Lake Pontchartrain. She watched children and adults take advantage of the warm January day. In New Orleans you could never tell what the weather would be like from one day to the next. It could be cold and bleak one day, and warm and sunny the next. That was why most New Orleanians never knew what a real winter was like. And Vanessa was one of them. She'd never been further north than Baton Rouge, the state capital, ninety miles away.

Across the street, Vanessa could see people fishing in the lake. As she watched, streaks of color appeared in the sky from the setting sun. It was beautiful. Her mind was on Scott. She wondered if she had made the right choice. It wasn't as if she hadn't walked away from other men. She'd never given it a second thought before. But walking away from Scott made her feel as if she was walking away from an important opportunity—one she'd never know if she didn't take a chance and open the book.

The sky was now dark, and the lakefront was emptying of families and filling with couples. How long had she sat there? Vanessa looked at the sky and spotted the first star. Now, how did that poem go?

Starlight, star bright, first star I see tonight

I wish I may, I wish I might

Have the wish I wish tonight...

Vanessa felt a little silly but made her wish for a second chance to meet Scott again.

CHAPTER SIX

Scott released a sigh of relief. The house was absolutely quiet. The girls had fallen asleep not long after they left the driveway of Burger King, and experience had taught him how to take sleeping children out of the car without waking them.

Just as he put his chair in a reclining position, the phone shrilled in the quiet house. Megan must have been playing with it again, because the ringer was on high.

Scott got to the phone just after the second ring, then wished he hadn't. It was Wendy. He wasn't in the mood for answering questions about that double-e woman. Remembering the predatory way she had looked at him, he felt only disgust. Then he recalled a pair of soft brown eyes with a frank, open look that caused an entirely different feeling.

"I heard you braved a trip to Storyland with the girls," said Wendy. "I'm proud of you, little brother."

Wendy knew his fear of taking the girls out alone, so it was good to hear the compliment. It made him remember that she was all the family he had left. When their parents died not more than a few months apart, they had become closer. Even more so after Kathy's death two years later, when he had moved to New Orleans, where Wendy had lived since her marriage to native born New Orleanian, Jack Cantrelle. But her constant matchmaking schemes were making him crazy.

"Scott, everything went okay, right?"

Realizing that his mind had wandered, Scott lied, seeing no reason to alarm Wendy after the fact. "Yes, it went fine. It's just that Storyland was exhausting, especially for me. The girls are napping now, and I was about to do the same."

"Sounds like a good idea, but first tell me how the shopping went this morning. Did you meet anyone interesting?"

"I wasn't going to mention it, but yes, I did." Scott purposely misled her into believing he had an interest in the double-e woman. Maybe then she'd back off a little. He meant the browned-eyed sexy woman with the long legs, Nessa.

"I knew you'd hit it off. I'm sorry I tricked you like that, but I didn't know any other way to get you to at least meet her. She's been crazy about you since she saw your picture." Hearing the excitement in her voice made Scott feel a little guilty, but not guilty enough to confess. Wendy went on, "You know, she reminds me of Kathy. She's the same size and build, and even has the same color hair."

Scott nearly jumped out of his chair in surprise. She was absolutely right. Nessa was the total opposite of Kathy— from the color of her skin to the lovely shape of her body. But he found her attractive, whereas Kathy's replica stirred nothing inside him. Nessa was tall, nearly as tall as he, and definitely not skinny. She had curves and plenty of them. He imagined tracing his hand along each and every curve, beginning with her full breasts, which had caught his undivided attention earlier, and moving down to her waist and rounded hips. Then he'd run his hands along the curve of her behind and move along the front to...

"Scott, for the third time, are you going to take her out?"

"What?" he asked as he slowly awoke from his daydream.

"A date, I said. Are you planning to take her out?"

Visions of Nessa in his head, he answered, "Yes, absolutely. When we meet again. It's fate, you know."

"Scott, are you okay?"

Now completely aware of the different tracks their conversation had taken, Scott wanted to get off the phone quickly. "I'm tired, Wendy. I just want to take advantage of this time—to rest while the girls are napping."

"Why of course, I understand. Just fill me in later, okay?"

"Okay, bye Wendy."

Scott hung up before he heard a reply. His brain was tired, but after his vivid daydream another part of his body was throbbing. The daydream continued as he fell asleep with a huge smile on his face.

CHAPTER SEVEN

Jimminy Cricket sure knew what he was talking about. Those wishing stars are powerful. Or was it just fate, Vanessa wondered as she watched Scott and a whole entourage of people, including his daughters, follow him into her pew.

Vanessa was sitting in the back pew because she knew she'd have to leave right after the final blessing to help serve the coffee and donuts the church provided after ten o'clock mass every third Sunday. Since very few people sat in the back, she was surprised to hear anyone entering. Then came the shock of seeing Scott looking right at her, smiling.

He walked up to her, never losing eye contact, and whispered, "Fate, we meet again."

Vanessa had no chance or desire to reply at the time. The church's organ boomed with the hymn "Let There Be Peace on Earth." And as the priest and altar servers walked up the aisle, Vanessa's shock drained away, and amazement took its place. She smiled thoughtfully. Yes, we meet again. There might be peace on earth, but Vanessa doubted if there would be any peace within herself with Scott standing so close to her.

She was right. There was no peace; her body was a riot of emotions. She was happy, relieved, nervous, and down-right afraid of the attraction she felt for a man she'd only just met.

Throughout the mass, Vanessa was intensely aware of Scott, and he definitely made sure of it. After the introductory prayer when the entire congregation sat, there seemed to be a space problem that caused Scott to have to sit very close to her. From shoulder to thigh, Vanessa could feel heat coming from his body. Then there was the Missalette Malady. Scott politely passed one of the prayer books to each member of his group only to find that he didn't have one to follow the mass. So he quietly asked her to share with him.

He looked meek, mild, and innocent. But Vanessa saw right through his ploy noticing that Vicki and Megan were also holding missalettes in their little hands. She pointedly looked at the girls, and then gave Scott an I-don't-buy-it smirk.

He defended himself by whispering, "I couldn't let them feel left out."

Vanessa shared but found her neck aching from trying to avoid staring at him as often as she felt his eyes on her.

During the homily, Vanessa listened to the priest begin his sermon by saying, "During the month of January we honor a man who spoke of brotherhood and love, Martin Luther King, Jr. If he were alive today he would be proud to see how this parish has embraced his teachings…"

Vanessa looked around as he went on with the sermon. He was right. This church did represent love and brotherhood. There were white, black, red, brown, and yellow people alike, coming together in this small parish to pray. They also worked well together, and just about everyone knew everyone else. As her gaze returned to her pew, Vanessa's eyes collided with Scott's. His look seemed to say, 'We belong together, listen to what the priest is saying. How can he be wrong?'

As the sermon ended, Vanessa dug into her purse for her weekly offering to help support the church. She felt Scott moving and wondered if it was necessary for her heart to beat so loud or for her stomach to turn into knots. He passed a dollar to each of his daughters to put into the basket before placing his own offering in the basket. Glancing down to the other end of the pew Vanessa realized how quiet the girls were. Were these the same children she had seen in Storyland yesterday? Suddenly Vicki noticed her and sang out, "Daddy, it's the brown lady again!" loud enough for the entire congregation to hear.

It felt as if every person was looking right at her, the only brown person in the pew. She saw many familiar faces turned her way in speculation. Vanessa just smiled and shrugged her shoulders. What else could she do?

Vicki was making her way to their end of the pew. And of course Megan followed, saying, "Hiya, hiya, hiya!"

Scott quieted them down, but another problem surfaced. Both girls wanted to sit next to Vanessa. She solved the problem by putting Vicki on one side and motioning to Scott to move down so there'd be room for Megan.

"Must I?" he whispered, but to avoid drawing any more attention, he gave in.

As he motioned his nephews to scoot over, Wendy and Jack both gave him questioning looks. Scott just grinned.

He watched his daughters leaning against Vanessa and was amazed at how quickly they came to like her. It was as if they'd met her months ago instead of just yesterday. He couldn't believe he had only just met her himself. Yesterday, he never would have guessed he'd be seeing her this soon. He said a prayer, thanking Wendy for urging him to come to mass and consider sending the girls to school here next year.

He'd been a Catholic all his life but hadn't set a foot in church since Kathy's funeral. It hurt too much. He'd lost both his parents before either of his daughters were born, and Kathy not long after. His little girls were not only missing the love of their mother but their grandparents as well. Scott had lost faith in God. But when he stepped into church again for the first time, his faith was restored, for who should he see but Nessa.

At first, walking through the doors of the church made him feel uncomfortable, like a hypocrite, following, but not believing. It was pressure from Wendy that had gotten him to come in the first place. She'd pushed the right buttons by playing on his concern for his daughters being raised in a Christian atmosphere. And the convenience because Wendy and Jack were joining this parish and sending the boys to school there anyway. They could take turns dropping off and picking up the kids. And then she hit below the belt, reminding him of the importance of setting a good example for his daughters. Wendy knew what she was doing. She knew how he felt about raising his daughters after virtually ignoring them the first year or so of their lives.

Still, as Wendy had led the group into church he'd hung back. Just as she had been about to settle everyone in a pew he whispered to Wendy to follow him and had led everyone to Nessa's pew. At that moment he became a believer and thanked God for bringing him back to church.

Sitting next to Nessa in church, listening to the priest's sermon, and watching her with his children, Scott realized that this was the woman for him. He'd only met her yesterday, but in his heart he knew. Now he had to convince her of that. He had a feeling that he had his work cut out for him.

CHAPTER EIGHT

Having endured Scott's effect on her long enough, Vanessa did something totally out of character for her. She left church before the final blessing right after communion, not even returning to her seat to say her prayers. It was like leaving home without getting dressed first.

Monica, who'd been watching her from across the church, followed her out, leaving her kids with their grandparents.

"So, Ness, that was him."

Vanessa continued to walk, with Monica keeping pace. "Yes, that was him."

They continued to the reception area, both lost in thought. Vanessa stopped and turned to Monica. "It was obvious, wasn't it? You could tell, couldn't you? I bet the whole church could tell!" she moaned, feeling so mixed up inside. She was trapped between feeling elation over her wish coming true and confusion about what to do now that it had.

"Yes," Monica said simply.

"What am I going to do? You know I actually wished for this on a star last night. It came true, and in church. God must be in on this too." Feeling totally bewildered, Vanessa wailed, "I don't know how to handle this now!"

"Don't! Don't handle it," said Monica. "Just let it happen."

"Let it happen?"

"Yes, let it happen."

Let it happen, that's what she was going to do, Vanessa repeated to herself as she poured cups of milk for the children who would be entering the reception hall any minute. Just because she found him attractive and wanted to get to know him didn't mean she was going to marry him or anything. That was the last thing she wanted.

She could get to know him as a friend—and his daughters, too. They were so cute and sweet that they brought out her never-ending supply of maternal instincts. She'd have to be careful for the girls' sake, and her own, to make sure Scott knew she wasn't getting involved in a serious relationship.

Vanessa began passing out cups of milk with a bright smile on her face. As she bent to get more cups from the cabinet that also served as a milk table, she heard a familiar voice saying, "Hey, brown lady!" Vanessa looked up to see her friend Joann, a fellow church member. "You know, I think the name's gonna stick."

"Get out of here, Joann," Vanessa laughingly replied.

"As a matter of fact, I will. I'm visiting my parents. We're having a big celebration, my brother is in town."

"See you, Jo."

Joann was right about the name, because many of Vanessa's friends came by, snickering, and addressing her as "Brown lady." Vanessa was glad her parents hadn't made it over to the milk table. She was a grown woman, but their concern for her always seemed to go overboard.

From across the hall Vanessa could see by the look on her dad's face that he was dying to know all. Her mom was probably having a tough time holding him back. Knowing

that she'd see him later today was probably what kept him
away from the milk table.

When Scott realized that Vanessa had snuck out on
him, he didn't feel like hanging around. "I don't want
donuts and coffee," he repeated for the third time as
Wendy maneuvered them into the reception hall. Scott
knew he was being childish but couldn't help himself. He
felt an intense sense of disappointment. He just wanted to
go home and wallow in it.

"Scott, what's the point of visiting today if we don't get
to meet anyone? Although it looks as if you knew at least
one person in church." Wendy waited for him to
comment, but Scott refused to part with any detail about
Vanessa.

Vicki, with the ears of a rabbit, had heard her aunt and
said, "Yeah, and she's real nice. I like the brown lady a lot."

Scott stooped. "I know she's brown, but it isn't polite
to keep calling her the 'brown lady.' "

"But what should I call her then?"

"Her name is Vanessa, so I think you should call her
Miss Vanessa, if you ever see her again."

"Can I have a donut now?" Vicki asked changing the
subject.

"Sure sweetheart." Vicki barely waited for him to finish
speaking before she was running across the room yelling,
"Miss Vanessa! Miss Vanessa!"

As Scott looked where his daughter was heading, his heart swelled with relief. Nessa. He hadn't lost her after all. Grabbing Megan's hand, Scott said to Wendy, "I told you I didn't want donuts and coffee. I'm going to have donuts and milk."

"But Scott—" Wendy began.

"Leave it be, Wendy," Jack told his meddlesome wife as they watched Scott head for the milk table. "It's obvious to me that your little brother can take care of himself."

"But I want to know what's going on."

"And you will, eventually. How about some coffee and donuts," Jack suggested as he steered his wife and sons in the opposite direction.

Vanessa smiled as she watched Scott approach with Megan in tow. She had to remind herself to take it easy as her heartbeat skyrocketed. She'd just finished talking to Vicki. It was decided that Miss Vanessa was too long, and that she could call her Miss Nessa. So it was to the tune of Miss Nessa this and Miss Nessa that, that Scott came upon them. He picked up two cups of milk and handed one to Megan and one to Vicki but kept his eyes focused on Vanessa.

"Hello, Nessa," he said, grinning ear to ear. "I thought I'd lost you."

"That's interesting." Vanessa stopped to clear her throat. "I've never been lost before."

"I thought you were—to me."

"Oh, I was just helping to serve the milk," she explained unnecessarily, irritated at the shaky sound of her voice. And did she have to sound so...goofy?

"You seem to have run out of customers," Scott commented.

Vanessa looked around, and sure enough, almost everyone in the hall seemed to have settled down at tables or stood around chatting.

"How about joining us for some donuts and milk?"

Vanessa was about to accept the invitation when she noticed someone approaching the milk table. It was the guy who, apparently with his family, had come to church with Scott and the girls.

He walked up to the table. "Don't worry about me. I can help myself. I learned how to pour milk in the army. They teach you all kinds of stuff there. Just ask Scott." He leaned closer. "He looks a little strange and all, but he's all right. He's from up north," he whispered, as if that said it all.

As he walked away, Vanessa asked with a smile in her voice, "So you're not a native New Orleanian?"

"That obvious, is it?"

"With the help of a stranger. That was someone you know, I assume."

"My brother-in-law, Jack."

"He seems a little strange. I guess the army could do that to you, all right."

"He's never been in the army. That's just Jack being Jack," Scott explained, not interested in talking about his brother-in-law. "So how about joining us for breakfast?"

"Please, Miss Nessa, please," begged Vicki.

Megan looked up, gave Vanessa a milk-mustache smile and sang, "Please, please, please."

"How can I say no?" Vanessa answered, knowing she was lost. Their dad was incentive enough.

Silently thanking his adorable daughters, Scott led them to a table, then went to get donuts from a nearby tray.

As Vanessa sat down, she felt a little conspicuous. She knew that Monica was probably watching her, and that her parents were somewhere out there too. And then there were all her friends who had gotten a kick out of the 'brown lady' episode. She was sure that they were all waiting for some kind of entertainment.

"You know," Scott began, interrupting her thoughts. "Besides the fact that you're a native New Orleanian, an Olympic grocery cart racer, a teacher, and a church-goer, I don't know a lot about you."

"You just about summed me up. And I think you know an awful lot about me considering how long we've known each other."

"A whole day, a lifetime, but tell me more."

"Well, I enjoy cart racing because I'm, maybe, a little bit crazy, but I rarely admit it. I love children, which is why I teach. And I go to church every Sunday because I believe in God. By the way, I'm part of the Welcoming Committee. Welcome to Saint Ann's Church."

"Thank you," Scott said, seeming to mean more than those two words implied. "But I'm sure there's more to know than that. I'd like to find out, if you don't mind. On a more personal level, that is," he added softly.

"I feel the same way," she quietly confessed. "But, first let me get something straight."

As if Scott knew what was coming and didn't want to hear it, he suddenly became interested in his daughters' hands. Well, maybe it also had something to do with Megan standing on a chair and launching herself onto Scott's back. And Vicki patting his leg in an attempt to get his attention. She left such a perfectly formed powder-sugar imprint of her hand that Vanessa wanted to suggest that he get it framed.

"I think they're finished with the donuts." Vanessa fished in her purse for her never-ending supply of pocket wipes. With all the nieces and nephews she had, Vanessa kept them handy.

With the clean-up of hands done, Vanessa looked around to see a deserted hall. "Everyone's gone."

Scott decided to take advantage of the situation. "Looks like my ride's gone. How about taking us home?"

"I could do that if you've really been deserted."

Scott put on a pitiful little-lost-boy expression. "My evil sister, Wendy, has deserted me."

"I heard that, Scott." Wendy marched across the room, intent on protecting her reputation. "I don't know what this crazy brother of mine is saying about me, but none of it's true. And since he doesn't seem inclined to introduce me, I'll do it myself. I'm Wendy Cantrelle, and this is my hus—"

"I'm her wife, Jack," Scott's brother-in-law interrupted. "And as you can see, she's just another one of those bossy Northerners. She's been here over ten years but still stands out like a sore thumb."

Throughout his little speech, Jack snuggled his wife close to him, softening his words with his touch.

Wendy responded by sputtering, "Wife! You are not my wife. Jack, what are you trying to say?"

When Jack only grinned, Wendy playfully punched him in the shoulder. The look of agony on Jack's face had to be phony because Vanessa could see a twinkle of mischief in his eye.

Happy to know who Wendy was, Vanessa introduced herself. "I'm Vanessa Lewis, and Scott did use words like evil and deserting when he mentioned you."

"Well, between the two of you, Vanessa will think something's wrong with me. And to think we just joined this church parish."

"Don't worry, Wendy. I have brothers just like them. And I never take them seriously."

"Well, I normally just ignore them." Wendy took a sleepy Megan from Scott's arms. Vanessa found it amazing how quickly Megan had gone from being a jumpy little jack rabbit to a tired little mouse.

Wendy made a face at Scott because he'd been so quiet throughout the whole exchange. "But sometimes it's hard to keep quiet and pretend they're normal."

Wendy announced to everyone in general, "The boys are outside playing. They saw the swing set and went wild. So I'm going to get back out there." Wendy grabbed

Vicki's hand and started for the door. She turned to Jack. "Why don't you show Scott to the rectory, then he can register if he wants to." To Scott she said, "Let the girls spend the afternoon with us. You can relax and enjoy a little quiet." This command, and it was a command, was issued as Wendy walked out the door. "I'd better go help my hus—oh, I mean wife with the kids."

"See what I mean, real bossy," Jack said with a grin. "Vanessa, why don't you show Scott around."

And before she could answer, Jack was out the door. Both of the Cantrelles were very good at giving suggestions that were actually commands.

Scott, who'd watched and enjoyed the easy camaraderie between his family and Vanessa, felt things were going along perfectly. He put on a pitiful face again and moaned, "You see, they've deserted me, again."

"What I see is that your very nice sister has given you an afternoon off. And I'd have to say that you have a very transparent family. I can see right through them."

"What can I say, they're only trying to help me out. So, will you be my guide, and can I still count on that ride home?"

"And why should I?"

"Because you're part of the Welcoming Committee of St. Ann's Church."

"This seems to be over and above the call of duty, but since you've been deserted, what else can I do?" she agreed, knowing full well she was going to take advantage of this opportunity to spend some time with him.

"You can spend the afternoon with me?" Scott asked hopefully.

"Sorry, I can't. I usually visit my parents on Sundays." Vanessa knew that this sounded pretty old-fashioned, but her family still gathered every Sunday to have a big dinner and spend time together. And if she didn't show up today, Vanessa knew she wouldn't hear the end of it. But, she thought, it was just as well since she wanted their relationship to develop slowly.

Scott's wistful expression made Vanessa wish she had the afternoon free.

"Oh, well, it was worth a try," Scott grinned. "Lead the way, Welcoming Committee."

As they walked across the church grounds to the rectory, Scott took her hand. It was such an innocent yet intimate touch. Vanessa had held many hands before, most of them belonging to small children. Scott was no small child. Her heartbeat accelerated when he gently squeezed her hand and she hoped her palms wouldn't become leaky faucets again. She couldn't believe how something so simple could be so exciting, and feel so right.

Vanessa waited in the outer area of the rectory while Scott talked to the secretary. The pastor, Father Brett, a very tall man with a deep brown complexion, bushy eyebrows and hair, came in to say hello when he spotted Vanessa. He was not only her pastor, but a family friend. He'd been a part of this parish longer than she could remember. Going to any church function wouldn't be the same without Father Brett being there. He even, on occasion, stopped by to have dinner with her family when his schedule allowed.

Scott came over and Vanessa introduced him to Father Brett. "Scott's a new member of St. Ann's."

"Oh, good and welcome," he said raising a bushy eyebrow at Vanessa. She knew what he was thinking, or rather hoping, since he was the priest celebrating mass today.

Everyone knew she was rarely interested in anyone, even Father Brett, and he looked as if he was delighted.

To Scott he said, "If you stick with Vanessa, you'll be in good hands." With that touch of wisdom he walked away, surprising Vanessa with a wink. This confirmed her suspicions about God bringing them together.

Walking to Vanessa's car, Scott announced, "I think I'm going to take Father Brett's advice."

"And what advice is that?"

"I'm going to stick with you. Got any glue?"

Vanessa smiled. "No."

"Honey?"

That sounded interesting, but Vanessa only grinned and shook her head.

"Syrup? Candy? GUM!"

"No. No. And absolutely not!" she got out as laughter escaped her. Scott was impossible, and he made her laugh. She liked that.

"I guess I'll just have to use my charm," he answered with a smile that revealed dimples she had never noticed before. They gave him a boyish look, but also added to his sex appeal.

That smile seemed to shout, "You can't resist me!" And Vanessa knew she couldn't. It didn't matter if he was white. She didn't stand a chance.

CHAPTER NINE

Pulling into the driveway of a two-story brick house on the lakefront, Vanessa was impressed. Scott must have a very good job to be able to afford a house in this area. One thing was certain, he wasn't a teacher. Teachers didn't get paid enough to live in such an upscale neighborhood.

"Thanks for the ride, Nessa," Scott said in a deep voice that sent chills down her spine. He made no move to get out of the car.

She loved the sound of his voice a little too much, so she tried to make the conversation light. "Just look at it as another helping hand from the Welcoming Committee."

"I'd like to think that it was more than that. You gave me a lift because you couldn't resist me. It's all part of the plan, you know." As he spoke, Scott looked into her eyes. He traced little patterns on the inside of her palm.

"What plan?" Vanessa squeaked.

"The plan I have to make you stick to me. Like super glue, the thickest maple syrup money can buy, and marshmallow candy."

"Why marshmallow candy?"

"It's the stickiest candy I can think of."

"Then you're not too confident in yourself. What happened to that charm of yours?"

"I'm still going to use plenty of that, this is just my back up plan," he told her.

"And why do you need a back up plan?"

"Just in case some equally handsome, excessively charming guy tries to steal you away before you realize that we were meant to be together." He didn't mean to say all that. It was too soon. The words just seemed to float out of his mouth. But Nessa didn't seem to mind.

"Oh well, then you'd better add the gum."

"The gum?" he asked feeling mesmerized by the movement of her lips. "Nessa?"

"Yes?" she asked. His tone made her forget the silly conversation they were having. The sound of her name, his name for her, in that deep voice, made her feel hot and anxious. For what?

"I'll just stick to the charm for now," he told her, gently brushing her eyebrows with a fingertip.

"Okay," she said as his finger trailed across her face to land softly, briefly, on her lips.

The warmth left from his finger made her stare at his lips. She knew what she was anxious for.

"Nessa?"

"Yes?"

"There's something I want you to do."

"Okay," was all she seemed able to say.

"For right now, I want you to forget the fact that I'm white and you're black."

"Mm," she answered still staring at his mouth. For a man, his lips were unusually full.

"Can you do that? We're just a man and a woman attracted to each other. Knowing that, will you give us a chance?"

She nodded her head, but Scott wasn't sure she'd heard a word. She looked like she was in a trance, and he felt the same way. Just touching her hand was making him crazy.

He knew that Vanessa had only to glance down to know exactly what she was doing to him. Gazing at her mouth Scott decided to put an end to their misery.

Vanessa must have come to the same conclusion because she seemed to meet him halfway. Their first kiss was simple, yet it was powerful. Scott didn't want to scare her off by letting his control slip. Slow, he reminded himself as he lightly touched her lips with his own, gently nibbling on them. It was torture, but he dared not trust himself to touch her in any other way, not yet.

Vanessa was in a state of wonder as Scott kissed her—wondering why she had waited so long to taste his mouth, wondering how lips so firm could feel so soft.

She wanted more. Much more. Bolder than she had ever been before, she slowly passed the tip of her tongue across his lips. This must have been the sign Scott had waited for. He gathered her into his arms and held her close, so close that not one ounce of air separated them. The kiss deepened, and then Vanessa became even bolder by slowly ending with another lingering caress across his lips.

She opened her eyes and found herself staring into smoky gray ones, and smiled with satisfaction.

Scott drew back a little. Her smile had to be the strongest aphrodisiac. And if this kept up, he'd have to invest in buying baggy pants because these were already confining and could possibly cut off his circulation. He kissed her once again. Gently and with wonder, sliding his hands up and down her back, he simply held her, waiting, hoping to come back to normal.

Vanessa, having never experienced such a kiss, was happy to find that Scott was affected too. The evidence was apparent since, in some mysterious way, she had ended up on his lap. She could definitely feel just how aroused he was. He felt hard and warm. Strange how it didn't bother her. Normally she'd be running away from such intimacy, but this felt right, and oh, so good. Too good!

"Nessa?"

"Yes," Vanessa sighed.

"What color am I?"

"Gray. Smoky gray."

"What?"

"You have smoky-gray eyes, Scott."

Scott laughed. "Thanks for letting me know. I'm relieved that you remembered my name."

"Oh, I know who I've been kissing, and I think I'd better be careful around you," Vanessa said, moving out of his embrace.

Scott reluctantly released her. "And why is that?"

"You make a girl forget her principles. I don't normally kiss on the first date, and look at me, we haven't even been on one yet. Not only did I kiss you, but I find myself sitting on your lap." Vanessa ended in a whisper and moved closer to the driver's side of the Explorer.

"But," she added smiling shyly, "I enjoyed it very much. And as color goes right now you seem to be a nice shade of pink."

Scott, worried and embarrassed when he realized that he might have moved too fast, was indeed blushing. And he couldn't remember the last time he'd done that. But her pleased honesty delighted him and made him fall even deeper. He knew he was falling in love for the second time in his life, and he couldn't seem to keep his hands or his eyes off of her. Capturing her hand and rubbing his thumb across her palm for the pleasure of touching her, Scott knew he had to see her again. Today.

"We can fix the date problem. Will you go out with me later today?

"I'd like that," Vanessa agreed.

"But I have to warn you that we'll have a couple of chaperones. The girls will probably be home by then. I hope you don't mind?"

"Not at all, Scott. It'll be fun." And safer, Vanessa added to herself, remembering the way she had been all over him a few seconds ago.

"Well, then tell me when and where I can pick you up?"

Vanessa named her address. She lived near City Park, a half dozen blocks from Bayou St. John, in a small apartment behind her landlord's house.

At his perplexed expression Vanessa realized he had no idea where she lived. Having pity on him, she suggested they meet at his house.

"I wouldn't mind spending the entire afternoon driving up and down streets to know exactly where you lived."

"That won't be necessary, I already know where you live."

"True enough, but I have no desire to sit around wondering if I'm really going to see you again. What if you suddenly changed your mind?"

"I won't," she promised.

That seemed to satisfy him because he asked, "Is four o'clock, okay?"

"Fine."

Scott got out and began to walk toward his house. On impulse he came back and unable to resist, walked to the driver's side and motioned for Vanessa to roll down her window. He leaned into the open window to give her a lingering kiss. "Now that's two dates I'm committed to," he whispered. "I feel obligated to make up for the kisses I stole today."

He stepped back and watched her drive off, assured by the look in her eyes that he'd see her later today. Scott whistled as he walked into the house.

CHAPTER TEN

Hearing the familiar sounds of talking, laughing, and music coming through her parents' front door usually brought forth feelings of happiness, comfort and excitement every Sunday. But today Vanessa was a little nervous. Even though her family loved her, they had a habit of teasing her unmercifully and minding her business. Of course this interference was not restricted to her. All her brothers and sisters were that way with each other, including Vanessa. It was their way of showing they cared. So she'd done her share of teasing and digging, too. But being one of the youngest caused her to suffer more. Before she could knock on the door or ring the bell, Vanessa's oldest brother Randy did the honors, causing her to wonder if he'd been waiting for her.

He shouted to everybody within hearing, "Hey y'all, look! It's the brown lady. Or maybe you've changed color since the last time I saw you." Looking at her nose to nose, because they were about the same size, Vanessa being the tallest female and Randy the shortest male in the family, he decided, "Naw, you're still brown. C'mon in, Ness."

Vanessa hugged him then gave him a little push. But before she could get five steps into the room, three of her oldest nieces, ranging in age from eight to ten, ran up to her. They'd made up a song. Knowing that her sister Tracy was responsible, Vanessa stood and humored them.

She's the brown, brown lady
And she is the best!
Oh, it's Auntie Ness!

Yeah, it's Auntie Ness!

They repeated their little song over and over, demonstrating some elaborate steps and moves. Vanessa knew they must have practiced since after church; it made her laugh. She hugged her nieces and shook a fist at Tracy, who was hiding behind a door. Vanessa made her way to the kitchen where she knew she'd find her mother, Monica, her two sisters-in-law, and her brother Warren. Warren was the baker in the family, and you could always expect a wonderful dessert being made if he was anywhere near the kitchen.

Her mom was stirring a big pot of gumbo full of shrimp, sausage, and crab. "You're late Ness, what kept you?" Joyce Lewis asked.

Monica walked over and gently elbowed Vanessa, as if to say, 'Watch out, here it comes.' She whispered, "We'll talk later."

Vanessa gave her mom a kiss. "I'm not really late, Mom, I just had a stop to make."

"And would that have anything to do with that man and what looked like his whole family we saw you with in church today?" bellowed a tall, dark-skinned man who normally could be seen with the same smile that was so much a part of Vanessa. But now there was only an ugly frown on his face. It didn't faze Vanessa; everyone knew it was fake.

Vanessa smiled at her dad as he stood in the doorway leading to the backyard. He usually took the direct approach to getting information, and he always thought that scowl of his helped him to get whatever information he was after. It worked when they were kids. Now it was just a pleasant reminder of her past misdeeds, not that they were many.

"Now Calvin, leave the girl alone. She just got here." Joyce gave her husband a look that made him frown even more.

Vanessa stifled a giggle as her father made his way across the room to his wife.

Slicing French bread, Ness absently watched as her dad stopped behind her mom to slide a hand around her waist.

"Now what was that for, Joycie?" he asked in a loud whispered.

"You know what you promised me not fifteen minutes ago. After thirty-eight years of marriage you should know that a hug and a kiss isn't going to get you out of it," Joyce told him sweetly.

"But, I didn't even kiss you yet."

"Cal, a promise is a promise."

"Yeah, Dad, a promise is a promise," Vanessa chimed in, positive that their discussion had something to do with her.

Her dad frowned up at her again then looked at his wife. "You have such sweet eyes, why are you using them to try to shut me up?"

"We've already talked about this, Cal," her mother whispered, moving to get the butter out of the fridge.

He followed her around the big kitchen. "Yeah, but you know, I don't like the way that man was looking at my baby girl."

A grunt, a smirk, and a couple looks of understanding were darted Vanessa's way. Everyone in the room had already experienced their father's help, advice, and unsolicited interference.

Joyce handed the tub of butter to Vanessa, pretending that no one heard her father's comment. "Don't put too much butter on that French bread, Ness. We don't need to clog up people's arteries any worse then they already are." Joyce walked back to the stove. Cal followed. Everyone stayed in the kitchen pretending to be absorbed with whatever task they'd been working on to help prepare dinner.

"I know what you're worried about, and I know why you're worried. Cal, you can't run your daughter's life," Joyce whispered back to him. But everyone in the big kitchen heard and knew exactly which daughter they were discussing.

"But I want life to be easier for my children, not harder," he told her, not bothering to lower his voice this time.

"Cal," she softly warned, turning away from her gumbo to stare at him.

He grunted but kept anything else he was probably dying to say to himself. Instead he turned to Vanessa. "And exactly why were you so late today, girl?"

Vanessa gave him a kiss on his cheek. "Sorry, Dad. I promise, if there's anything for you to worry about, or anything to tell, you'll be the first to know."

"At least he goes to church," Calvin told her, catching a comment from Warren.

"I sure would like to know what's going on around here!" Warren demanded. "I went to eight o'clock mass this morning, and missed everything."

"There's nothing to tell, he's just someone I met yesterday."

"And he followed you to church the next day with his whole family?" questioned her dad.

"And what's this I hear about you hitting him with a grocery cart, Ness?" Warren's wife, Jackie, asked.

"Ness!" Joyce paused in the middle of adding file to the pot of gumbo. "You're not still doing that cart racing, are you?"

Warren laughed. "No wonder he tracked you down in church. He was probably trying to see if you had insurance for cart racing. You might have a lawsuit on your hands."

Everyone else joined in the laughter, even Vanessa. Just then, one of her nieces came in, singing the song they'd made up, and Vanessa didn't feel like laughing anymore. She knew keeping her secret was a losing battle in this family.

Sonya, Randy's wife, said, "I'd sure like to hear about all this excitement."

With the "brown lady" song ringing in her ears and a room full of questioning faces turned on her, Vanessa promised, "I will tell everything, after dinner. Now, what else can I do to help, Ma?"

Having kept her promise—with the eager help of Tony, Jasmine and Mark—Vanessa sat patiently through some good-natured ribbing, then said goodbye to everyone in general, and stole away. She got as far as the front door before she was stopped by her mother's voice.

"Vanessa, wait, take some gumbo home. Go on to your car, I'll bring it out to you."

If her mother had called her Ness instead of Vanessa she would not feel like a ten-year-old about to be trapped for an interrogation. Her mother couldn't possibly know that there were some parts she had left out of the tale.

When Joyce got into the car, Vanessa knew she was about to get an earful of whatever was on her mind. As she waited for her mother to start, Vanessa took a good look at her. Her complexion was very fair, a contrast to her dad's dark skin. Which in turn created a rainbow of browns in the family. Vanessa had never really thought about it because it was never an issue in her family. She knew that to some people skin color was important, but with the Lewis family, it was never a big deal. Maybe that was one reason Scott appealed to her.

Placing the plastic container of gumbo carefully on the floor, Joyce wasted no time. "I came out here to talk to you, Vanessa, because I'm a little worried. I was always happy that you put off having any kind of serious relationship until you finished school and were pretty much settled. But today, watching you at church and at the hall today, I have a feeling there's a lot going on here."

"Ma," Vanessa began, not wanting her to go on.

But Joyce did go on. "I'm not going to preach to you or tell you what to do. Just be careful, and take your time. I'll see you next Sunday, if not before." With that being said, she went back into the house.

Vanessa drove off, thanking God for such a wonderful mother. Her parents had always supported her. Vanessa knew she'd have no problem in that direction, but it still felt good to hear her mom confirm what she already knew.

Getting home at three o'clock gave Vanessa very little time to get dressed. It was beginning to get cold again, and a sweater and jeans seemed like a wise choice. The weatherman had been right for a change. A cold front was headed this way.

After showering and trying on every sweater she owned, Vanessa, for the first time in her life, wasn't pleased with how any of them looked on her. Seeing that it was already three-forty, she started to feel desperate. Why did everything look so wrong? Then she remembered a new vest she'd bought with Looney Toon characters all over it. With a long-sleeved shirt, it would look great. Grabbing her Looney Toons cap from the closet and putting her black Bugs Bunny tennis shoes on, Vanessa was finally ready. Looking in the mirror, she thought, "Casual." That was what she planned. After all, this wasn't a real date. Not with two little chaperones coming along. She adjusted her cap and headed out the door.

Three-thirty and fresh from the shower, Scott realized he didn't have anything clean to wear. He'd forgotten to stop by the cleaners and he'd told the new babysitter house-keeper not to bother with the laundry because it was her first week on the job. He'd been more concerned with the girls getting used to her than clean clothes. Scott had planned to do some laundry himself this weekend, but he hadn't done so much as one load. His mind had been so full of thoughts of Nessa, there was no room for something as mundane as washing clothes.

Jeans, Scott thought, he must have at least one pair of jeans. He went into the washroom. It was supposed to be a casual date. After all, Nessa believed the girls were coming along. He'd thought so too until Wendy called to say they were begging to spend the night. Since tomorrow was a holiday celebrating Dr. King's birthday and Wendy didn't have to go to work the next day, the arrangement was perfect. It couldn't have turned out better.

That was not all she'd called to tell him. Wendy had related to Scott a conversation she'd had with the double-e woman.

"I thought you told me you were going out with Dee Dee?" she asked.

"Well…"

"I certainly hope you aren't," Wendy interrupted. "She left a strange message on my answering machine, and when I called she told me she wouldn't have a thing to do with you."

"Oh yeah." Scott laughed with relief because the feeling was mutual. "Did she say why?"

"Dee Dee said it was because you went around with 'that kind of woman.' "

"That kind of woman?" Scott was confused.

Sounding upset Wendy said, "She told me, people like the 'brown lady.' Then she went on talking about the purity of the white race and some other trash. I just hung up on her. Amazing, isn't it?"

"Yeah," Scott answered, astounded that someone had judged Nessa as inferior because of her color. The double-e woman had never even met her.

Nessa was even more of a woman than he originally thought when he'd compared them physically. Nessa, he sensed, was a woman with deep thoughts and feelings. He could feel it in the way she kissed him. Scott knew, even before she admitted it, that Nessa didn't make a habit of kissing and hopping onto the lap of just any man. But Miss Double-E had looked as if was ready to attack him right in the store. She was as shallow as a person could get.

"To think that I was trying to set her up with you. Sorry, Scott, sometimes you don't really know a person. She looked like Kathy but was nothing like her."

"But sometimes you do know a person," Scott answered, thinking about Nessa, "before you really get to know her."

"That's true, too." Wendy paused. "You feel that way about Vanessa, don't you?"

"It shows?"

"Of course." Wendy sounded indignant. "I'm your big sister, and I'm supposed to notice these things. And I give you my blessing. I like Vanessa."

"Thank you!"

"Have fun on your date. And, Scott, sorry about Dee Dee. I don't know if I can stand to work with her now."

"No sweat, and I intend to have a ball." He smiled into the phone. "I love you, sis."

"Me too, bye."

What a sister, Scott thought. Talk about luck! Now he'd get to have Nessa all to himself.

His mind on clothes again, he spotted a pair of jeans sitting atop the washing machine. They were the same ones he'd worn yesterday. They were his only hope. He couldn't go out with Nessa on their first date wearing sweats, which were all he could find in his closet besides the suits he wore to work everyday.

Scott sniffed the jeans and checked for smudges. They seemed decent. He decided to freshen them up by sprinkling a little baby powder inside, but what he did was shake a lot of baby powder inside. He shook them and was suddenly surrounded by a cloud of baby powder. Hacking and coughing from breathing in the powder, Scott went in search of a shirt.

Opening his closet, he spied a sweatshirt with Bugs and Daffy playing basketball. Wendy had gotten it for him, saying it reminded her of when he and Jack played. Reluctantly putting it on, Scott hoped that Vanessa wouldn't laugh at his choice of clothing. Finally dressed, Scott looked at the complete mess he'd made of his bedroom. Normally a very neat person, he hated leaving his room like this, but there was no time to clean it. And since there was no chance of Vanessa seeing it anytime soon, he couldn't care less.

The doorbell rang as he was running a comb through his hair. Dying to see Nessa, he quickly went to the door, opened it, and burst out laughing. He was so worried about what he was wearing, then Nessa appeared covered from head to toe with Looney Toon characters.

Vanessa's gorgeous brown eyes widened. "What's so funny?"

Loving the perplexed look on her face, Scott pulled her inside. Wanting to explain, but unable to resist, he kissed her. He kissed her eyes, her nose, her cheeks, her chin, every available part of her face. Watching her confused expression change to one of pleasure, he said. "I knew we belonged together. We even dress alike."

Not giving her a chance to see for herself, Scott proceeded to kiss her like he'd been imagining all afternoon. Besides, it gave him an assurance of many future dates. He whispered in her ear, "Another kiss, another date. I'm adding them up."

"And I'm keeping count," Vanessa told him.

As the kiss deepened, Scott removed her cap by running his fingers through her hair to trace her ear. His body was trying to convince him to back her onto the sofa, peel away her clothes and—

His mind ordered him to stop. Now. It was too soon for that. He knew he was falling in love, but Nessa hadn't figured it out yet. So he must be patient. Before he could act on his resolution, Vanessa drew back.

Cursing himself for coming on so strong Scott said, "I'm sorry. I mean—did I upset you?"

"No, it's not that." She paused. "Where are your daughters?"

Relaxing now that he knew what was worrying her, and pleased to see the concern she had for what his daughters might have witnessed, Scott couldn't help but tease her a little.

"I used them as a ploy to lure you into my clutches and have my way with you."

"I see," she said. Vanessa stationed herself behind a large leather sofa in the middle of the room. Even though she believed he was kidding, she didn't trust herself with him without the kids around. She had been alone with him less than an hour earlier and barely resisted him then. And if he hadn't stopped just now, they probably would have ended up on that big black sofa or on the floor. So, what would she do if he really wanted to have his way with her? Give in? Probably? Definitely?

"And what if I don't want you to have your way with me?" Vanessa asked trying to convince herself of that.

Scott sat down on the sofa. "Then we'll go out to eat a famous New Orleans style dinner and have a great time."

Surprised at his change in demeanor, Vanessa was intrigued. She wanted to sit down and talk with him; joke and play with him; kiss and make love with him. *Whoa, stop it girl.* It was a good thing he couldn't read her mind. Noticing a strange look in those gorgeous smoky-colored eyes, she wondered if he could.

Sitting down next to him on the sofa and searching for a safe topic, she noticed his sweatshirt for the first time. "We really are dressed alike."

"Yup, like I said, we belong together."

"Our clothes, yes. Us, maybe," she answered with a smile. "I wore my outfit hoping to impress Vicki and Megan. Where are they?"

"Wendy kept them. They didn't want to come home. Besides, I like what you're wearing."

"Thanks, I like what you have on too."

"Great. So, why don't you show me the sights? I've lived here less than a month and only visited a few times. I'd like to see more of the Big Easy. I just love that nickname."

"I'm game if you are, but first, you must understand that Bourbon Street is not the only street in the French Quarter," she informed him, relieved but also disappointed that they wouldn't be completely alone for the rest of the evening.

Settled in Scott's car, they headed toward the French Quarter in comfortable silence. As they drove down Elysian Fields Avenue the buildings began to change when they neared the historic area.

"We're all pretty unique down here, and it's all tied to our past," she said. "Louisiana is a real melting pot. There's a mixture of the original French and Spanish, who brought in African slaves. I bet you didn't know that not all black people in New Orleans were slaves. There was a large population of free men, and women of course, of color. After the Louisiana Purchase, other people from different nationalities settled here, too.

"Really, that sounds very interesting."

"I know, I sound like a history book, but it excites me. Learning about how people lived then makes me understand a lot about how things are now."

"I like history myself. And I love anything that excites you," Scott said, displaying his dimples.

After that crack Vanessa laid it on thick, attempting to bore him. But it backfired because Scott really was interested. He seemed to actually like history. So Vanessa went on to talk about slaves and how many of them in New Orleans were skilled laborers and how they contributed to the architecture. They drove past the French Market and Jean Lafitte's Blacksmith's Shop where, it was said, he conducted his notorious pirating business. Then there was the statue of Andrew Jackson in the middle of Jackson square. He fought in the Battle of New Orleans with the help of Jean Lafitte and his pirates. These were only a few points of interest that she shared with him.

Remembering her mother's advice and trying to give him food for thought, Vanessa launched into another round. "Ever heard of Quadroon Balls?"

"Nope, can't say that I have, teach."

"Quadroons were free men or women with at least one fourth black blood."

"One fourth black blood? How do you measure that?"

"Well, I think that if one grandparent out of four was black, you were a quadroon. Anyway, these young black women would attend a special ball so that single, rich white men could meet them and choose them as mistresses. It was accepted that these young white men could sow their wild oats before they settled down. You don't have any wild oats left to sow do you?"

"Naw, with Vicki and Megan I have my hands full. My life's wild enough for me right now. I don't have enough energy left to do any more sowing. Most of the time, after I put them to bed, it's lights out for me, too."

She could imagine the trouble the two lively little girls probably gave Scott when he tried to put them to bed. After witnessing the way they'd run circles around him in Storyland, Vanessa felt a little sorry for him. "So no wild oats?"

"Definitely not."

"Now stop me if I'm wrong, but it's not so much that you don't have any more wild oats. It sounds more like you're just too tired to go sowing," Vanessa summed up for him.

Scott laughed. "Let's just say that maybe I have just enough for one particular woman," he answered, squeezing her hand. "Yes, I think I have one wild oat that needs to be sowed on a regular basis. Care to help me out?"

"Let me think about it," she said, enjoying his playful mood. But she was determined to see how he felt about certain issues. "Let's get back to the Quadroon Balls. There were more black women than white back then. Some couples would stay together for life. A few of them even ran away to France or Cuba to get married. A lot of them had children, of course."

"Of course, it was bound to happen with all that sowing going on."

Vanessa grinned, then stopped herself to gauge how he was reacting to her monologue. All she could detect was quiet interest mixed with his humorous remarks. "Interesting, isn't it?"

"Very, what else can you tell me?"

"Their children were octoroons. I don't know if you've noticed yet, but down here there are many shades of black. And it's mostly due to Quadroon Balls and the matches they led to. It was something like a common law marriage. But then, when a couple broke up, a large sum of money was given to the woman, including money for any children. Wasn't that just too much? And this was considered normal!"

"Normal or not, it doesn't matter because I like your shade."

"What if I was darker?"

"I wouldn't care."

"Or lighter?"

"It wouldn't matter. Nessa, it's you I couldn't keep my eyes off of. It wasn't your color that first attracted me. What I mean is, I couldn't miss the fact that you were black anymore than you can miss the fact that I'm white. But your color, or difference in color, isn't what attracted me. It was your eyes." That wasn't entirely true since his first view was from behind. But maybe he'd let her know that part later, much later.

"Really?" questioned Vanessa. Because he'd voiced her own feelings exactly, except his eyes weren't the first thing she'd noticed. "I feel the same way."

"Good," Scott answered and pulled over to park, surprisingly near the French Market. It has been the place to shop in the French Quarter for over two hundred years. You could find anything from fruit to purses, souvenirs to hot sauce, and of course anything that was "naturally Na'wlins."

Scott turned to her and took both her hands in his, making sure he had her undivided attention. "I've always thought that what was inside a person was most important. And from the moment I looked into your eyes I could see what kind of person you are. That's what attracted me. Your loving, caring eyes. And what I've seen for myself so far confirms what I believe."

Thinking about the double-e woman, Scott went on to say, "Some people appear to be something they aren't. Nessa, you are just what you appear to be. I want to find out every aspect I've only just begun to uncover. And it has nothing to do with your outer covering."

More at ease since she understood him a little better, Vanessa laughed and pointed out more sights. "I think it's all amazing, I didn't even know all this history until I was forced to take a Louisiana history course in college. Then you couldn't keep me out of a library. But enough of the lecture, I want you to see the wrought iron balconies, and the St. Louis Cathedral. It's the oldest in the country."

They continued their walking tour with Vanessa as the guide. She held Scott's hand and pointed out everything she found fascinating. At first she was very conscious of the people around them, but most paid them no attention, so it was easy to ignore the few strange looks they got once in awhile.

After eating shrimp and oyster po-boys at Maspero's, they strolled to the Moonwalk to watch the last rays of the sun go down over the Mississippi River. It was beginning to get even colder; the cold front was moving in pretty quickly. Scott sat on the steps above Nessa and wrapped his arms around her, sheltering her from the wind.

"It's actually beginning to feel just a little bit like winter here," Scott whispered in her ear. "Are you cold? Are you ready to go?" he asked, squeezing her tighter.

"Not unless you want to." Vanessa smiled breathing in the moisture laden air and the scent of...baby powder? "I'm enjoying myself."

Further down, on the Moonwalk, a saxophone played a beautiful soft melody. Not knowing the name of the tune, but enjoying the music, Vanessa relaxed against Scott. He snuggled her closer. It felt so good and so special that she thought nothing could intrude upon their closeness until they both heard a very loud, very drunk voice bellow out behind them.

"Do you see that! He's huggin' and touching all over her. Ain't you afraid to get your hands dirty?"

Vanessa and Scott turned around to see two white men stumbling toward them. They both looked like linebackers.

One guy seemed to have a little sense and sounded a bit more sober. He mumbled to his friend, "Hey man, leave those people alone," as he pulled him away, which was no easy feat.

As he was being dragged away, Mr. Big Mouth let out one last parting shot at the top of his voice. "Hey man! Take my advice…stick to your own kind!"

Never having had to deal with such blatant bigotry before, Scott was slow to react, but the shock quickly wore off. Indignation took its place. He yelled back, "I'm sticking to the human race. And I hope to God that you're the last of whatever species you call yourself!"

Mr. Big Mouth obviously heard and was trying to make his way back, but his friend was able to keep him moving in the other direction. Scott was glad. He wasn't afraid for himself but Nessa. There was no telling what the men would have done to her if they had knocked him out.

People around them were shaking their heads in sympathy. Someone tapped Scott on the shoulder and in true N'Awlins accent said, "You gotta ignore those kind of people, man. They're just plain ignorant."

Scott shook his head in agreement, grabbed Nessa's hand, and pulled her away. He had to talk to her. She hadn't said a word or looked at him during the whole incident.

Opening the car door for her, he could see that she was still shaken. After getting into the car he tried to draw her out. "Nessa?"

Finally focusing on him, Vanessa let out a sigh. "Scott! I couldn't believe it! They were huge, and that ugly one with the big mouth, he looked like he could stomp us both into the ground. I was so scared!"

"Are you okay, now?"

"Yeah I'm fine. I'm sorry. I guess I was so worried I froze. But I knew, if he came any closer, instinct would have taken over. I would have been able to help protect us. I took a course in self defense a couple of years ago. I could have dodged around to distract him while you came in for the kill."

"Dodging and distracting, huh?" he asked in amazement. "What about the things he said? Did they bother you?"

"Oh, that? He's a jerk, Scott. Not everyone thinks like that. Although I'll admit I was leery and a little worried about how I'd react to an incident like this. But I overcame that fear ten minutes after being out with you."

"What about the strange looks we were getting?"

"People are curious and nosey. We're an odd couple to them."

Scott held Nessa in his arms and kissed her tenderly. "You amaze me, Nessa. I thought I'd be sitting here for the next half hour trying to convince you to go out with me again."

"I'm not discouraged that easily. Besides, I liked what you said. The part about sticking to the human race, and I agree."

"I'm, glad to hear it. Now how about finishing your job as tour guide, miss. You have one more sight to show me."

"And what's that?"

"I need to know how to find your house. I spent all afternoon looking for it. I won't tell you how many times I got lost."

CHAPTER ELEVEN

Turning over and peeking at her clock, Vanessa wondered what could have woken her up at seven o'clock in the morning. It was too early to get up, especially on a Monday—a Monday that was a holiday. And whatever it was, she thought with disgust, it roused her from an incredible dream. She had been dreaming that she really had run over Scott at the grocery store, knocked him inside the cart, and took him home. She was just unpacking him and putting him away, not in the kitchen with the other groceries, but in the bedroom, when she was so rudely awakened.

Boom-boom-boom-bam was the noise that had her jumping out of bed and nearly out of her skin. She was definitely wide awake now. Her heart was pounding, and not knowing exactly what the noise was or where it had come from had her standing frozen in the middle of the room.

Boom-boom-boom-bam! "Ness!"

There it was again, coming from her front door. Those voices, Vanessa knew without a doubt who they belonged to. The banging started again, this time more elaborate. The simultaneous shouts of "Ness!" at the end were the last straw. Grabbing her robe, Vanessa marched to the door. She moved so fast that she barely had time to get one arm into a sleeve before she got to the front door. She swung the door open and demanded of her younger brothers, "Exactly what do you think you're doing?"

"Coming to have breakfast with you, sis," John answered, punctuating each syllable with a beat, and then turning on an innocently straight face.

"And--uh, Ness, we might be nice enough to give you some lessons on how to dress. It's not too hard," Josh teased, holding up the dangling half of her robe.

Vanessa gave them a frosty stare that lasted about ten seconds under the boyish looks they cast her way. It was no use. She knew they'd make their way over here sometime today, obviously getting the scoop on Scott after she left Sunday.

"Oh, get in here and be quiet. What were you trying to do, wake up the whole neighborhood?" Before they could step inside, Vanessa noticed that someone else was disturbed by the noise. She smiled, knowing full well that they deserved what was about to happen to them. "Now you've done it." She stared pointedly at the fence that separated her landlord's backyard and the neighbor's around the corner. "You've got more than you bargained for."

"Oh, no!" John moaned, glancing behind him.

"Not her!" Josh hid behind his brother. "Man, John, you shouldn't have beat on the door so hard. You woke up 'The Pest.'"

"The Pest" was Vanessa's neighbor—a teenager with more hormones than sense—a teenager with a huge crush on both her brothers. It seemed to Vanessa that the girl couldn't decide which one she was in love with. After all, they were identical twins.

"Quick, Ness, let us in and lock the door!" Josh begged.

"Too late, here she comes," John announced in a voice full of doom.

Sabrina Adams, her neighbor, the Pest, gracefully hopped over the low wooden fence, tightly holding onto a large package. It would probably be her excuse for coming over.

It turned out to be a box of candy. Sabrina positioned herself smack in the middle of the brothers. This was no easy feat. Knowing Sabrina too well, they had formed a human wall against such a move. But showing no subtlety whatsoever, the Pest trade room for herself.

"That was some leap, Sabrina. I think you're getting better," Vanessa commented, having seen Sabrina in action before.

"Ten years of gymnastics," she boasted, trying to impress the twins. "Good morning Josh, John," she sighed, turning to each with a dreamy expression.

"Mornin' Pest," John answered with a grin. Even though he'd avoid an encounter with Sabrina like the plague, he tended to treat her like a bratty little sister. They both did.

"Hi 'Brina," Josh muttered, not concealing his annoyance as well as John.

"So what's up, Sabrina?" Vanessa finally asked, purposely waiting, watching and enjoying the sight of her brothers squirming under Sabrina's dreamy gaze.

"Oh, I'm selling candy for school. Wanna buy some?"

"It's seven o'clock in the morning!" John told her, doing his best to sound astounded.

"Oh! So you two do know what time it is." Vanessa let them know they weren't totally in the clear. "And your timing was awful. You interrupted what would have been the best dream I ever had in my life when you started banging on the door."

"We'll make it up to you. See, breakfast!" Josh explained, pointing to a paper bag full of muffins that had gone unnoticed. "Sorry, 'Brina, gotta go. John and I are here to help save Vanessa." Motioning for John to follow him inside, he asked. "Dreamin' about him, huh Ness? John, it's worse than we thought, get in here!" he called over his shoulder.

But John pulled out a five-dollar bill. "Here, Sabrina, eat some for yourself, on me."

"I can't," she moaned. "I break out."

"With that beautiful face?" John complimented, then quickly stepped inside.

Vanessa promised to buy some candy later, then closed the door. "That did not help you one bit, John. It'll only encourage her."

"I had to say something, since Mr. Rude here hurt her feelings. Well, it's done." He headed for the kitchen counter. "And we didn't come here to talk about the Pest. We want information. First hand information."

"Leave me alone, guys."

John let out a whistle. "You're right Josh, she's serious. She's finally fallen."

Slowly walking toward Vanessa, Josh started one of his speeches. He sounded like a Baptist preacher. For someone who never set foot in a Baptist church, he was pretty good at it, and today he was really on a roll. "Unbelievably, Vanessa Lewis is in love!" He repeated, "Yes, in love!"

Josh, the music man, hummed an accompanying melody. He sounded like a well-tuned organ. "And not with just anyone. No, not just anyone." The humming became more dramatic. "Not for Ness. Not just any man would do. She's fallen for…" Josh gasped, "a white man!" He gripped his heart with both hands and fell to knees. The humming ended.

"Will you two cut it out? I swear, are you ever going to grow up?" she asked as she stepped over Josh to make coffee.

"I don't plan on it." Pointing to Josh, John added, "And I can guarantee you he never will. So, when do we get to meet him?"

"When you both finally decide to grow up." Vanessa shook her head. "The way you're both acting now you'd scare him off. He'd want nothing to do with someone with such crazy relatives."

That said, Vanessa figured she'd shared enough of her love life with her little brothers and refused to say another word about it. When they realized they weren't going to get any more than what they already knew from their other sources, they gave up and enjoyed an early-morning break-fast with their sister.

Vanessa loved her brothers, but sometimes they made her crazy. From the moment they came home from the hospital with her mom, they had stolen her heart and made her crazy. Vanessa was five years older, so she saw it as her duty to protect them from bullies at school and being teased too much by their older siblings. In return, they adored her. She had no doubt that they were nosy, but deep down she also knew they were practicing their mother-hen tendencies toward her. Not that they'd admit it, though.

After an hour spent laughing and enjoying each other's company, Vanessa decided it was time for them to go. They had a parade to go to, and Vanessa had a bed calling her. She directed them out the front door.

"Thanks for breakfast," she told John, giving him a hug more for his concern than the muffins he'd brought.

John got into the driver's seat. Josh paused and quietly told her, "All joking aside, we really want to meet this guy."

"Yeah, he has got to be something for you to react the way we heard," John added, "And to be so closemouthed."

"Bye, guys." She nudged Josh toward the open passenger door and followed to make sure he got inside.

"Don't try to protect him too much longer." Josh growled, hanging out the window. "If you make us wait too long, we might be forced to reveal to him the true nature of the Lewis family, and who knows what could happen then."

Knowing Josh, Vanessa could just picture it. She smiled and wondered what Scott would think about her crazy little brothers.

She hugged the half of Josh that was hanging out of the window, and told them, "Stop worrying about me and my love life. Go find some girls to torment. I'm just your sister."

"We know," John said, "But we can not help it. It's our job—" John stopped mid-sentence, spotting Sabrina in her backyard the same instant Josh did. "Aw, man, Josh, let's go, now! It's the Pest, again!"

Vanessa laughed and waved them off. Her plans for the day were to lounge in bed until lunchtime. She was invited to go to the Children's Museum with Monica and the Jones crew later, their treat.

It wasn't until she was nearly at the door to her apartment that Vanessa noticed Scott sitting astride a ten speed bike. He was staring at her. She was surprised and happy to see him. Her body's reaction to him was working overtime just in case her brain was too slow to register how happy she was to see him. Her heart, her palms, her legs were all doing things that were not normal for her, each part remembering the way he kissed and held her on the Moonwalk.

She smiled.

He didn't.

He didn't say a word. He just sat there, staring, looking sad. Something was not right. He looked so forlorn. She shyly walked up to him, making her wobbly legs move to stand right in front of him. Vanessa grabbed the handlebars, a foot on each side of the front wheels to steady herself

"Good morning."

"Good morning," he answered gruffly. No sign of the pleasant man she spent time with last night was present. Gone were those adorable dimples and that special light in his smoky-colored eyes. He seemed uncertain and...disappointed?

He said, "I see you've already had company this morning. I'll just be on my way."

"Wait a second, you can't leave already."

"I think I need to go." His hands tightened on the handlebars. "I'm not any good at handling what I just saw."

"And what did you see?"

"You standing here, wearing a short robe, an extremely short robe."

"And…?"

"And two guys standing here with you full of smiles and freely touching you."

"Scott, you're jealous!" she told him, happiness in her.

"No I'm…" He scowled. "I am."

"I like hearing you say that."

"I couldn't help but admit it."

"I have something to confess, too." Vanessa's hands inched toward his. She slowly covered both of his hands with her own. "Those guys were touching me, and I admit to touching them. It's called a hug."

"I know. I saw."

"What you don't see is that I was giving them sisterly hugs. Those were my baby brothers, Scott."

"Good." Scott grinned. "I wouldn't mind being kicked out like that," he stated, displaying those dimples that were absent but a minute before.

"I'm not so sure I'd want to kick you out." Oh, she was getting bolder by the minute.

"Then invite me in," he suggested, eyeing her attire. "I could help you get dressed."

Suddenly remembering what she had on, Vanessa felt very self-conscious. "You probably mean undress." She shook a finger at him. "I told you, you're dangerous. Bye-bye," she said, pointing to the sky.

Scott looked up to see a few fluffy white clouds in an otherwise clear sky.

"There go my principles and willpower. They floated up to that cloud the minute I saw you, and now the wind's taking them away."

"I can't say that I'm sorry," he whispered, leaning closer. "You smell delicious."

"It's lotion—peach scented." About to take him up on that silent promise of a kiss, Vanessa paused, spotting Sabrina still in her backyard. Not wanting an audience or to encourage Sabrina in any way she said, "All right, then. You can come in. I can offer you some coffee and a blue-berry muffin."

Before she finished speaking, Scott had put the kick-stand down. "Let me warn you, that by inviting me in you're asking for a repeat of last night's kiss."

"I realize that."

"It was more than reason enough to ride over here so early in this morning. All night, you were all that I could think about, Nessa."

"I know how you feel." Everything was moving too fast again. Vanessa turned to go into her bedroom. "I need to change."

Scott reached for and gently grabbed her hand.

"Scott?" She stared at their entwined fingers. The contrast surprised her because not once had she thought about their difference in skin color since last night's inci-dent. And then she looked into his eyes and uttered not a word of protest when he gently pulled her toward him.

A shiver of anticipation went down her spine as he captured her lips in a gentle but thorough kiss, being true to his promise. More shivers raced down her spinal cord and transformed into waves that spread and moved through every pore of her body.

Vanessa moved closer, pressing against him. She needed to share this feeling with him, needed to know he was feeling the same way she did. Feeling his hardness and warmth, she sighed with satisfaction. Oh yes, Scott felt exactly the same as she did.

They ought to stop right here and now...only Scott was nibbling on her bottom lip tempting her to open up to him again. She was tempted, already melting against him as if she was snow falling to the ground on a hot summer day.

Somewhere, somehow, she found the willpower at last to turn her head, resting it on his shoulder and effectively ending the kiss. A kiss that would have gone on forever, it seemed. She stayed in his arms savoring the feel of him, and Scott seemed content to have her there.

Just when she had herself under control, Scott whispered, "Nessa," and did something to her ear. She never thought the feather light brush of a tongue could make her whole body explode with pleasure. And her ear of all places! Feeling more than a little panicked, she pushed away from him.

Covering her ear in wonder and backing away, Vanessa stared at Scott. "Wow." She shivered and said again, "Wow! I'm...going...to...get...dressed."

Scott smiled, watching her head to the back of her apartment where he assumed her bedroom was. She walked backwards the entire time, staring at him. Vanessa probably felt that she had to keep her eye on him, just to make sure he didn't follow her to finish what they had started. He understood the expression on her face. He recognized it because he was experiencing it, too—complete and total arousal—everywhere. His nerve endings were tingling from the tips of his fingers to the roots of his hair.

Aware of the silly grin that must be pasted on his face, he sank into a nearby chair. That was unbelievable, even better than last night and ten times better than their first kiss the day before. Was it only just yesterday that he'd kissed her for the first time? He really was in love, he realized, his grin nearly splitting his face apart. It seemed the more he got to know her, kiss her, the better it felt. But now he had better behave if he didn't want to be kicked out.

Making it safely into her bedroom, Vanessa opened her closet door and looked at herself in the full-length mirror. She was shocked to see how disheveled she looked. Her hair, which she had brushed straight while her brothers were there, now looked wild. Her robe gaped wide open and revealed the short, nearly transparent pink nightie she'd worn to bed.

She couldn't blame the man for wanting to kiss her. She was amazed that he didn't attempt to do more. She quickly dressed, trying not to think about the "more" that they didn't do. She put on a pair of jeans. Then, as she pulled a navy blue sweater past her ears, she paused to press her hands against them again. "Who'd of thought?" she wondered aloud.

Not wanting to keep Scott waiting, Vanessa simply brushed her hair again, adding some hair spray to keep it from flying all over the place since hot curling it would take too long. She didn't want Scott wandering into her bedroom looking for her. A few moments later she walked into her small kitchen right off the living/dining room to see Scott putting water into a Sylvester teakettle. She liked the way the sweats he had on made him appear masculine and fit. They were made for comfort, but certainly let you know there was some man underneath.

He smiled at her. "You really do like the Looney Toons."

"Most definitely." She was glad but also a bit disappointed that he had chosen such a safe topic. "Sylvester was a gift from my sister Monica and her kids. You met them, remember."

"How can I not remember the near collision at the supermarket?"

"Will I ever live that down?" She took down two mugs. "I hope you like coffee with chicory. It's the only kind of coffee I drink."

"We'll find out."

They settled down side by side on the sofa to drink their coffee, both lost in thought. Both trying to think of something to discuss besides this amazing physical response to each other.

"Nessa," Scott began.

"Scott," she said, then rushed on when he paused. "I want you to know that I didn't expect to react so..."

"Irresistibly?" he asked, when she couldn't seem to find the right words.

"No," she laughed. "I was thinking more or less shamelessly. You seem to do things to me. I can't explain it, and I'm certainly not used to it," she said, feeling her ears tingle under his interested gaze.

"I noticed, and you're not the only one," he confessed, reaching over to caress her ear.

Vanessa caught his hand after the first stroke. "I want to take things slowly, Scott. We've just met, and I don't want to rush. I'm really just an old-fashioned kind of girl."

Looking into her beautiful eyes and seeing the earnest expression on her face, Scott knew he'd agree to anything as long as he could be with her.

That being settled, Scott planned on monopolizing her morning and possibly her entire day. He had to pick up the girls around lunchtime, so his whole morning was free. Maybe he could convince Nessa to spend it with him, and the rest of the day with the girls, too. He had the whole day off—despite a debate from his boss's son about the necessity for closing the office for this particular holiday. Travis Sr. had nipped his son's protest in the bud. Scott was pleased that he had the day free to spend with Nessa. He'd honor Dr. King by working on uniting the races in a more intimate way.

"Got any plans for today?"

"Monica and the kids invited me to the Children's Museum." When Vanessa saw his face change from inquiring to disappointment, she added, "I promised to go with them."

"An all day thing?" he asked, trying not to sound disappointed. Now why did he think she could possibly be free? Scott could tell that her family meant a lot to her. This was the second time she mentioned an engagement with them.

"Not until lunchtime." Vanessa knew she could probably weasel out of going, but the kids were counting on her coming, and she didn't want to disappoint them. When she made a promise, she kept it, especially promises made to kids. "Scott, why don't you and the girls come along? Monica won't mind. Jasmine, Mark, and Tony seemed to hit it off with your girls the other day at Burger King."

"If you're sure your sister won't mind." As if he cared. Scott was not missing out on this invitation. He had an unexplainable need to be with her. Even with almost half a dozen kids along. It didn't matter.

"No, I'll call and tell her right now."

While Vanessa went to use the phone in the bedroom, Scott decided that the problem he now had was not getting kicked out like her brothers were earlier. It was barely nine o'clock, what could he suggest they do together that wouldn't break his promise to take it slow? His mind understood her request and readily complied. Other parts of his body, on the other hand, were not as understanding or as easy to persuade.

"It's settled," Vanessa announced, coming back into the room. "We meet for pizza at twelve, and go to the Children's Museum straight after."

"Sounds good to me, but I have a problem."

"Wrong time?"

"No, too much time."

"Huh?"

"I have too much time on my hands, and I need to find some way to spend it wisely."

"Mm-mm, got any ideas?"

He saw a ten-speed bike hanging on a hook in the far corner of the living room. "How about a ride to City Park. I'll push you on a swing." He grinned. "We could even ride double."

Vanessa had done that many times before, with her nieces and nephews. But there was a distinct difference between a tot sitting on her lap facing her as she pumped higher and higher on a swing, and Scott swinging with her in what would be a very intimate position. Vanessa couldn't help but ask, "And who'd sit on the bottom?"

"Me, of course," Scott answered reasonably, showing that dimple and displaying his charm again.

Vanessa couldn't help but picture it in her mind and blushed at the idea of even trying.

Noticing and correctly interpreting the reason for the blush, Scott quickly lifted her bike off the hook and started out the door with it before she could change her mind. Vanessa swung a small canvas backpack onto her shoulder stuffed with a half loaf of bread and two bottles of water. Before she locked the door, Scott asked if she wanted a jacket.

"I'm okay. It's pretty warm out with the sun shining so brightly. I guess that cold front wasn't all that they thought it would be. This is New Orleans in January. Don't you just love it?!"

What I love is you, woman, he wanted to say, but he realized that declaring his love wouldn't fit in with the slow moving approach Vanessa wanted.

They rode out with Vanessa in the lead, straight down a street that intersected with Bayou St. John. Riding along the bayou they would run alongside City Park. They rode around and then through the park, ending up racing each other. It was fun. Feeling the breeze caress her face, the excitement of just being with Scott was everything she'd hoped she'd feel one day with the right man. Vanessa couldn't believe that just a few days ago she was wondering if she'd ever find someone she liked past the first date. Well, here was what she'd technically consider her second date, and she was well beyond like. Vanessa peeked over her shoulder and poked her tongue at him, daring him to catch up.

Scott responded to the dare, and also to the incentive for the other things he could possibly do with that cute tongue poking out at him. He pedaled faster, reaching her side in no time. Scott reached over and slowly lifted her hand off the handlebar.

Vanessa simply held on tight, afraid of losing her concentration, her balance, and of course her dignity by falling off the bike. This man could do things to her body without much effort at all.

When Scott began swinging their hands in the air, back and forth, just like a couple of kids, Vanessa relaxed and enjoyed herself, her fear of falling evaporating with Scott's more casual touch. Not that she remained unaffected, that wasn't possible.

To Vanessa, his touch was like an electric magnet pulling her toward him and holding her there as a steady stream of an electric current passed between them.

The park was nearly deserted, except for a few joggers. They came to a curve and had to drop hands or they both would have lost their dignity in the middle of the street. Vanessa led Scott around the perimeter of the park where neat and carefully maintained shrubbery formed the words CITY PARK. They rode toward the lagoon that ran through the park. Vanessa hopped off the bike and, feeling like a kid, grabbed a handful of acorns. She hid behind a tree for cover and pelted Scott with as many as she could fling. He kept coming, not even bothering to protect himself.

"Hey! You're supposed to fight back!"

"I will!"

"With acorns, it's an acorn fight!"

"You fight your way. I'll fight mine!" he answered, finally deciding to dodge the acorns.

Grabbing another handful of the small brown nuts as she ran, Vanessa tripped over the root of a huge oak tree.

"Oh no!" she shrieked as Scott pounced.

"There will be no mercy!" He pinned her to the ground with his upper body and held her hands high. "I must have revenge for all the injuries I've suffered under your hands."

"Injuries? Those were just little acorns!" She laughed, wiggling under him.

"Yes, but you caused me great pain, so I must seek revenge! Do not move, it will only make matters worse for you," Scott declared in a menacing voice that squeaked, ruining the effect. Having Nessa beneath him and at his mercy was indeed causing him to suffer.

Vanessa choked on her laughter trying to hold it back. "I can't take it anymore. Just give me my punishment."

"Okay, but remember, you asked for it," he warned in a deep voice that wasn't frightening at all. Besides, Vanessa anticipated and was eager for her punishment. She knew that for every prick, tap or brush of an acorn he would return a caress, a kiss, or the gentle brush of his lips.

Slowly his mouth came closer...but never reached its destination. Vanessa was shocked to see a small, stooped gray-haired lady beating Scott on the back with her purse.

"You leave that young lady alone, you beast! Go away! Can't innocent people live in peace!"

The woman was landing quite a few swings onto his head and shoulders. Vanessa stared in shock. Scott put his hands up in self-defense.

"Hey lady, wait!" he shouted.

"Run, young lady, run before he comes after you again. I got the beast." The woman kept right on hitting Scott as she tried to shoo Vanessa away.

Vanessa finally moved into action. "Wait! Don't do that he's my..." And just what was Scott to her?

"Tell her, Nessa!" he yelled, trying to dodge the sprightly old lady and her purse. That purse must have held bricks, or brass knuckles or something. "Help me please!"

The old lady, totally concentrating on her prey, took a breath to yell at Vanessa again, "Get, I said, young lady!" Get!"

Vanessa moved to stand between them in an attempt to save Scott. But not quick enough because the woman let go with a mighty swing directly into Scott's stomach, winding him. He fell to his knees.

With a satisfied grunt, she told Vanessa, "Well, get a move on. I got him down for you."

Vanessa knelt down beside him.

The woman's expression suddenly changed, "Are you crazy helping him? He attacked you!" she yelled, her voice as mighty as her swing.

Before the woman decided to start swinging the purse at her, Vanessa explained, "No, you got it all wrong, he wasn't hurting me. He's with me, and he's—he's mine."

"But you're...and he's..." the old lady sputtered, staring at both of them. "Well, I'll be," she said, walking off as if nothing ever happened.

"Are you okay?" Vanessa asked. Feeling sorry for Scott, she rubbed his shoulders and kissed his forehead.

"No," he answered, appearing to struggle to catch his breath. "I have to slowly recover," he wheezed. "I think large doses of kisses and some tender loving care every few minutes will do the trick. And in about a week..."

"A week?" she laughed.

"Yeah, then I might finally have my strength back."

Having seen glimpses of this humorous side of him before, Vanessa went along with him.

"Well, Mr. Doctor/Patient, this will have to do for now." She leaned forward and covered his face with kisses, then moved away when he tried to grab her for more.

"Watch it, Scott. Another old lady might come to my rescue," she teased him.

He jumped up, searching for any signs of the militant granny. Satisfied that none was in sight, he slowly backed Vanessa up against another oak tree to deliver her unfinished punishment, beginning with a little kiss on her earlobe.

Vanessa looked around, not being able to move back, she was trapped. "You know," she said trying to distract him, "City Park has the largest natural standing of oak trees in the world."

"Interesting," he said, moving to the other lobe, clearly distracted, but with her ears!

This distracting business took too much concentration. Vanessa gave up and was simply thankful to be leaning against one of those sturdy oaks. Otherwise she'd have collapsed.

"Whoa, that was almost worth being attacked for," he whispered in her ear, his breath caressing and doing absolutely nothing to help her withstand the tremors moving through her body.

"Almost?" she whispered.

"I'm so battered and bruised, I think I need another dose right now. And remember I'm yours. So you have to take care of me."

"You're mine, huh?"

"You said so, Nessa, remember? I heard it with my own ears," he answered smugly.

"I may have said something like that, but I was in a panic. I was trying to save you, so almost anything might have slipped out of my mouth."

"Oh, no, you can't deny it. I heard you. You said it, and you meant it. And as far as that saving part goes, you took your time about rescuing me. But you did come through in the end—a little late, but it was worth it."

"Why?"

"Because I've found out exactly how you feel about me. And it's a good thing, too."

"And why do you say that?" she asked, not wanting him to think too much of himself.

"Because you're mine too, Miss Nessa." It wasn't I love you, but Scott was glad to share some of what he felt for her. "Now, how about that other dose of medicine?"

Enjoying this brand of medicine herself, Vanessa took over and delivered one lengthy, thorough remedy for his aches and pains. Realizing this could go on forever without either of them wanting to stop, she finally ducked under his arms before Scott could stop her.

Remembering her backpack, she came up with the perfect distraction. "Come on, Scott, let's feed the ducks."

"Ducks?"

"The lagoon, the ducks, those creatures making all the noise. They're right over there." She pointed and pulled him in the direction of the loud quacking sounds.

Scott simply let her pull him along. "I'm an injured man, drag me where you wish. I will show no resistance to anything you might have in mind."

"What I have in mind is feeding the ducks."

That was perfectly okay with Scott, he just enjoyed teasing her.

So they fed the ducks, and drank the water she had brought along. Vanessa helped the invalid onto his bike so they could ride back to her apartment where she supplied him with another dose of "medicine," knowing he was going to milk his injuries for all they were worth. But she didn't mind, since she was enjoying the remedy herself.

Here was a man as crazy as she was. And he was winning her over with his charm. Scott made it easy to know him, tease him, touch him. What was it Monica said? "Let it happen!" Well, it was definitely happening, and a whole lot faster than Vanessa thought. Scott rode off and promised to be back within half an hour with the girls.

After being stuffed with pizza and running all over the Children's Museum with Jasmine, Mark, and Tony, Vicki and Megan declared it, "The bestest, most favoritest place to be." Scott thought having Vanessa with him was the bestest, most favoritest thing to have. Not just because he loved her company, but because she kept Vicki and Megan in line as soon as they set foot into the museum.

Just before Megan tried to shoot off on her own, Vanessa very firmly laid down the rules, which was really just one rule. "We all stick together, if not we all leave." Monica's kids nodded their heads in confirmation when the girls looked from Vanessa to Scott, to them.

"Don't worry," Jasmine confided, "it's just a safety rule to make mommies and daddies feel better. Can we go shopping first, mommie?" she asked Monica. "You can punch the buttons to pay for the food. It's fun," she told Megan and Vicki.

And Scott discovered that it was indeed fun, and much more relaxing with the safety rule in place. The highlight of the visit was the re-enactment of the famous Atlanta Boycott beginning with Rosa Parks refusing to give up her seat on the bus. The audience got to participate, so all the kids held signs as protestors. They loved it.

Scott took Vanessa's hand and whispered, "I'm glad we've overcome this obstacle in society. If we hadn't, I'd probably never have met you."

Those quietly spoken words took her breath away. She squeezed his hand in agreement.

CHAPTER TWELVE

Going to Nessa's house became an enjoyable routine every weekend. Scott and his daughters were becoming an integral part of her life. Their weekends were full and began every Friday evening. They'd go on trips to the park, the Children's Museum, of course, and Audubon Zoo to name a few. They even experienced movie night with Jasmine, Tony, and Mark.

Sometimes Scott and Vanessa actually got to have an evening alone, but the opportunity didn't occur too often. Most dates ended with the two of them relaxing and quietly watching a rented tape after the girls went to sleep. They got a kick out of renting videos they felt they could relate to. They discovered a mutual love of Motown and listened to his collection of tapes along with other oldies from the fifties and sixties, including the Beatles.

Their routine included going to mass together on Sundays at St. Ann's. Vanessa would then visit with her family with a promise to see Scott and the girls later that day. Every Sunday, she held back from inviting them over. Vanessa wasn't sure if Scott was ready to meet her family. She wasn't sure if she was ready for him to meet them yet either. Her parents often stopped to talk when mass was over. She could tell they really liked Scott because both her mom, and amazingly her dad, refrained from pumping Vanessa for more information. Vanessa figured this was her mother's doing because her dad always acted as if there was something he was dying to say. Too bad the rest of the family wasn't as reticent. They teased her because she was dating Scott, had been dating him for some time, and showed no sign of stopping anytime soon. They wanted to know why she hadn't "dumped this one, too."

Sometimes Vanessa wondered why she put herself through the torture of visiting every Sunday. But she knew the answer to that. It wasn't torture. If she didn't have this chance to visit with her family once a week, then Sunday just wouldn't be Sunday. And so she bore the teasing with a smile. She knew her family had no problem with skin color. It was just that they were all dying to meet the guy, any guy Vanessa finally seemed to be interested in.

And she was more than interested. Vanessa was in love with him. Scott was all she thought about. Writing spelling words on the board in class one day, she found his name in place of all the words beginning with "s". It was embarrassing to have six- and seven-year-olds giggling at you and asking what a "Scott" was. And listening to one wisecracking little second grader announce, "Miss Lewis needs to buy some Scott tissue." The whole class thought this was hilarious. It took a good five minutes to calm the children down. But still, days later, Vanessa would hear someone whisper 'Scott tissue' and hear giggles following the whispered words.

And if that wasn't enough, making love to him was all she thought about. Resisting him had become harder and harder. If he knew how often she wanted to experience more than those satisfying but unfulfilled moments in his arms, Scott would be shocked.

She was shocked; this was her body she was talking about. Having remained a virgin this long, Vanessa never thought she'd have to deal with this much temptation. Her few experiences with men had not prepared her for dealing with Scott. She'd smugly thought she had excellent willpower. Ha! She just didn't have Scott to resist—sexy eyes, body, and a rear end that...well, enough said.

Still, she was taking her time in this relationship. Vanessa was not rushing into any intimacy. Besides, they'd known each other for barely three weeks. It just seemed much longer.

Vanessa left her parents' house this particular Sunday with her newly discovered love for Scott fresh on her mind. So she built up her willpower, reinforced it with determination, and was ready to resist the power of Scott.

She pulled into his driveway to find him waiting for her. Did she hear a crack in that wall of willpower she'd just erected? He was leaning against a wide, white pillar in front of his house, waiting. Waiting for her. His hands were in his pockets. His eyes, dark, smoky, intense, were on hers. Something told her the girls were nowhere around.

She sat in her car and drank in the sight of him through the closed window. If looks could melt glass, the window would be gone. Scott was wearing a pair of tan dress slacks with a pullover sweater in cool earth tones and tiny splashes of blue. They molded to him in such a natural way that the quality of the clothes matched the quality of the man.

As she stared, Scott responded with a lift of his eyebrows. Vanessa didn't think they were going to Storyland or the Children's Museum today. In her mind, she heard a loud thunderous crack. This time, there was a huge gap in the foundation of her willpower as Scott pushed away from the pillar to open the car door.

"An afternoon of pleasure awaits us, Nessa," he said as he held her door open.

Pleasure? A riot of possibilities burst through her brain, causing her limbs to freeze. Talk about double meanings.

"Nessa?"

"Yes?"

"If you get out of the car one of these pleasures can begin immediately." Scott took her hand and drew her close to his side. The car door slammed.

Vanessa jumped.

"What's wrong, Nessa? Nervous?" he asked with another rise of his eyebrows and a grin that brought forth that boyish dimple.

"No, it's nothing," Vanessa answered, thinking the slamming of the car door sounded exactly like her willpower crashing in a cloud of dust.

As soon as they were inside the house Scott closed the door and pulled her into his arms. "Pleasure number one," he whispered. "A welcoming kiss."

A kiss? He meant a string of kisses that had an unbelievable beginning and an everlasting end. They left a trail of tingles up her arm, stretching across her neck, and reaching from one ear to the other, finally finding a place at home, on her lips.

Vanessa had a tight grip on his shoulders nearly pulling him down to draw him closer. His lips were moving down—down her neck. Oh that felt so good. Her fingers were itching to touch, to share with Scott some of the feelings she was experiencing. She reached behind him and slowly, shyly, moved one hand under his sweater, then the other. His skin felt so warm and male. She moved her hand up and down his back feeling his muscles contract as he moved.

He pulled her closer, and she could feel just how aroused he was. He placed kisses down the open V in the blouse she wore to church today. Church? Principles? Intimacy?

Suddenly the phone let out an earth-shattering ring. Vanessa jumped back. Scott raced to answer the phone before the next ring caused their eardrums to explode. Megan again, he thought. Moving the phone up high did not stop her fascination with the instrument.

"Hello!" he yelled, out of breath and full of frustration.

"Scott, it's me, Wendy."

"Oh, hi Wendy, sorry about that." He couldn't be mad at her. If it wasn't for Wendy he wouldn't have Nessa all to himself today.

"I hope I didn't interrupt anything."

Scott grunted.

"Okay, I guess I did. I wouldn't have called, but you promised the girls that they could talk to Vanessa. I've been holding them off for half an hour."

"You held out that long?" he asked, realizing he'd forgotten all about calling.

"Yes, and it could have been longer if Vicki didn't know how to tell time already. You told her three o'clock and she's been asking ever since."

"I know I promised." He sighed. "I hadn't realized it was that late, we were preoccupied."

"I can imagine."

Scott ignored the comment. "I'll get Nessa."

He thought that maybe it was good that the phone rang. He hadn't meant for things to go so far. When he said a welcoming kiss, he'd meant a welcoming kiss. He must show more restraint. Nessa would think he was a wild animal.

Scott turned to find her standing right behind him.

"Did I hear you say the call is for me?"

"Yes." He enjoyed the sight of her fresh from his kisses. Her hair always tended to be all over her head by the time he finished kissing and caressing her sensitive ears.

Scott looked down. She had forgotten to fix one thing. He reached over with a light, soft caress making a path down her open blouse. "You might want to button up." Her skin was so soft. So much for showing restraint, he thought.

She blushed and quickly turned away to button up. What she was dying to do was unbutton the rest of her blouse. But what she wanted to do and what she needed to do were two different things. No intimacy, not yet anyway. That was what she had forgotten earlier. Willpower, ha! She hadn't stopped; she wasn't going to stop. The phone stopped them.

The phone.

"Who is it, Scott? I didn't give out this number to anyone."

"My daughters. They were very upset when I told them I was going to take you out today while they stayed with Wendy. I promised them that you would call to say hello. I just didn't get around to telling you that yet," he sheepishly admitted.

"So, we're going out? Just us?"

"Pleasure number two."

Vanessa shivered. If pleasure number two was anything like pleasure number one, she was in trouble.

The receiver was suddenly filled with noise.

"I think they're waiting for you," Scott said.

Vanessa talked to the girls and promised to see them as soon as possible. They were such sweet little girls. She was already very attached to them, and the feeling seemed to be mutual.

Scott told the girls goodbye and reminded them to behave for their Aunt Wendy.

Before they left the house, Vanessa eyed his attire again.

"Care to tell me where we're going?"

"Pleasure number two?"

"Yes."

"How does a matinee at the Saegner sound?"

"A musical?"

"*Cats*. Have you seen it?"

"No," she answered.

"Good, I was hoping you hadn't. I'm sorry about the last minute notice, but Wendy grabbed the girls again and ordered me to take you on a real adult date."

"Wendy, huh?"

"I was all for it. You see, it will be my pleasure to escort you to the theater this afternoon."

"When does it start?"

"In about an hour."

"Scott, look at me! I'm not ready! Look at you! You're gorgeous!"

"Thanks for the compliment, but I think it fits you better. Since you're worried about the time I'll volunteer to help you dress." The eyebrows lifted and the grin that always appeared when he teased her was there once again.

"No, thank you. What you could do is meet me at my apartment in thirty minutes. That's thirty minutes. Don't come a minute sooner," she ordered.

"Are you sure?"

"Positive!"

Vanessa drove off and got home in record time. She quickly showered, and toweled down, trying hard not to think about Scott and her body's reaction to those pleasures he was dishing out. It took some deep concentration because her body was still tingling all over

Vanessa threw on a short slip, the material cool against her skin. She was applying some light makeup when she heard a knock on her door. Vanessa glanced at her watch—that wasn't thirty minutes!

She knew Scott would come early, but she wasn't going to let him charm his way inside. She was enjoying those pleasures too much.

Vanessa walked to her front door.

"Nessa, it's me, open up!"

"I know it's you, Scott Halloway. And you're going to sit right out there and wait. I'm not dressed yet."

"Then you'd better let me in. It's obvious that you need my help. We're going to be late if we don't leave soon."

"No, thank you. We'll be leaving soon enough."

"Okay, but I'm ready and willing if you change your mind."

Vanessa didn't respond but went back to her bedroom not wanting Scott to know how much his suggestion affected her. Having a vivid imagination didn't help. And hearing his deep laughter as she walked away only sent more chills down her spine.

She pulled out Old Reliable, a navy-blue after-five dress she'd worn on the few occasions she needed to dress up. It had a deep V down the front and short flowing sleeves. She looked at herself in the minor as she straightened out the dress that came just to her knees. Her eyes widened. She looked sexy. She didn't remember looking sexy in this dress before. Her eyes were drawn to her breasts. She pulled on the bodice. It slid right back down, revealing just as much as before.

Vanessa grabbed a navy blue and white scarf and tied it around her neck, positioning it directly over her breasts. There was another knock on her front door. Time was running out. They would be late if she didn't get moving. Vanessa untied the scarf, threw it on her bed, and went to the door. The scarf had looked ridiculous anyway.

She heard voices on the other side. Scott's deep timbre, and a lighter voice—Sabrina? Vanessa opened the door. Sabrina was keeping Scott company.

"Oh, there she goes, Mr. Scott." Sabrina got up from one of the patio chairs in front of Vanessa's apartment. "You look just too good, Miss Vanessa."

Scott's eyes first took in her face, and were pulled to and could not seem to move away from the deep V in her dress. It took awhile, but his eyes finally moved up again.

Scott had a feeling of déjà vu. This had happened before, oh yes, in Burger King. But this time the look in her eyes held no warning. It was a mirror image of his own—full of desire.

"Oh, you two look perfect together," Sabrina said pulling them closer together. "Looking at the two of you, I'd say black and white go good together." When neither adult responded Sabrina asked, "Right Miss Vanessa?"

"Definitely. Thanks for keeping my date company."

"No problem. He looked a little nervous and lonely out here. Be nice to him Miss Vanessa."

"I will," she promised, turning to leave.

"Miss Vanessa, I was wondering if Josh or John were anywhere around. You guys wouldn't be going on a triple date would you?"

Was that jealousy she heard in Sabrina's voice? "No, it's just us."

"And we'd better be going," Scott interrupted, just now realizing how long they'd been standing here. Not that his time was wasted. From the moment Vanessa stepped out the door he'd been marveling at the fact that this beautiful woman wanted to be with him.

"It was nice meeting you, Mr. Scott," said Sabrina. "And thanks for taking those magazine subscriptions. Oh, one more thing, don't forget those tips I gave you."

"Sure thing," he told her.

"Tips?" Vanessa asked.

"I'll tell you about it later," Scott promised.

"Y'all have a good time," Sabrina called. "And if you see Josh or John anywhere around tell them I said hi!"

Scott grinned as he watched Sabrina hop across the fence. "You have a nice little neighbor there."

"She's too much," Vanessa answered, her body responding to the hot look in his eyes. "But shouldn't we be leaving now?"

"Let me finish pleasure number three."

"I hope it doesn't involve going inside."

"No, it's the pleasure of appreciating the sight of my beautiful date," Scott said, leaning forward to press a kiss on her lips.

That night they made it up to pleasure number five, at least by Scott's counting: a welcoming kiss he recalled in detail, an enjoyable afternoon at the theater, admiring her beauty, dinner at Houston's on St. Charles Avenue while they watched the street cars pass by, and quiet but stimulating conversation.

Five pleasures. But no more intimacies. When the time was right, they'd be worth the wait.

CHAPTER THIRTEEN

Mardi Gras season had begun, and Vanessa hoped the excitement might distract her from the many pleasures she thought about indulging in with Scott. Mardi Gras itself was one big party, and it would be a pleasurable and safe experience, with no intimacy.

About two weeks before the main event on Fat Tuesday, barricades could be seen waiting on the sidewalks to be used during the parades, and bleachers displaying the traditional purple, gold and green colors of Mardi Gras were being constructed all over the city. There were more policemen on the streets and excited children in the classrooms. These were all obvious signs of Mardi Gras Fever.

Scott had never experienced Mardi Gras before and couldn't see what all the fuss was about. Vanessa decided to educate him. For the first lesson, she took Scott, Vicki, and Megan to a day parade.

Loading the mini cooler filled with drinks into the trunk of his car, Scott complained. "I don't see the point of standing in a crowd of people to catch beads and silly trinkets that you could buy in a store. Why don't we just go to Mardi Gras World and see the floats that artist guy Blaine Kern has built. And then, maybe to that other place, Accent Annex. Then we can buy the stuff ourselves."

Attempting to get him to understand Vanessa reasoned, "We can go to Mardi Gras World, later. There's a whole lot more to Mardi Gras than that. It's not just about catching beads and trinkets, but about trying to catch the most while getting caught up in the excitement and being a part of the crowd. It's about admiring and counting the floats, and watching the parade krewe all dressed up in their costumes. This parade might not be as colorful and big as some others we'll see at night, but it'll still be fun. And I haven't told you about the bands."

"I'm sure you will." Grinning, Scott leaned against the car. He was enjoying the sound of her voice and the movement of her hands as she talked.

"High school bands are really competitive down here," Nessa said. "And since you plan on living here for good, you may end up marching in a few of these parades right alongside Vicki and Megan. So you may as well see what it's all about."

Scott moaned at the thought, then checked to see if the girls were watching. Listening to Vanessa made him want to indulge in another pleasure. He tried to steal a kiss, his hand slowly moving up her hips, passing her side and slowly inching toward her breast. He almost reached his goal but was interrupted by the Megan song. "Daddy, Daddy, Daddy! Miz Nessa, Miz Nessa, Miz Nessa, go potty!"

"I'll do the honors," Vanessa volunteered. "You come too, Vicki, just in case."

Scott watched them go into Nessa's apartment. He smiled, remembering the tips Nessa's little neighbor friend gave him about being a good date. They were more or less a warning. Her exact words were, "Be polite and a gentleman at all times. And don't you dare take advantage of Miss Vanessa. She's the nicest lady in the world."

Everyone loved his Nessa: her neighbor, her brothers, her sister, her nieces and nephews, Vicki and Megan, and especially him. He wondered if Nessa was ready to hear that yet.

Scott glanced back at her apartment, wondering what was taking them so long. With Megan and her antics he could just imagine. He thought about going in to see if they needed any help. The girls would probably ban him on sight, preferring Nessa's help whenever she was around.

Scott had been inside her apartment a few times since his first visit but rarely stayed long, with the exception of movie night. That night, he found five kids to be a good buffer for his lustful thoughts. If he spent more time there without the children nearby, his dilemma of how far was safe to go with Nessa before he exploded would have been solved by now.

It had been years since he last dated and over a year since Kathy died, but he could still tell when a woman wanted to be in his arms. And Nessa wanted to be there. But she also wanted to take their relationship in slow stages. He'd never push her and was allowing her to set the pace, but Scott knew that if he pushed the right buttons Nessa would probably beg him to make love to her.

What a nice fantasy, he thought. It was just too bad for his raving hormones that he wanted more. He wanted to build a strong relationship with her first.

Hearing Nessa and his daughters, Scott looked up to see them racing to the car. Nessa made a face, pretending to trip and fall so the girls could win. They saw her tumble to the ground and ran back to her, thinking she was really hurt.

"Oh, my Nessa's hurt!" Vicki shouted, hugging her.

"No, my Nessa," Megan yelled, grabbing her by the arm to stake her claim.

Vanessa showed them that she was okay and explained that she was both Vicki's and Megan's Nessa.

"Are you really my Nessa?' asked Vicki.

"Yes, of course," Vanessa answered.

"My Nessa, too, too, too," Megan got in.

"Certainly."

Loving the way she handled his daughters, Scott wished they were a family right now. And maybe Vicki and Megan knew something, because from then on she was known as MyNessa, which sounded more like MaNessa with an emphasis on the Ma.

That afternoon Scott became a parade maniac. They went to the day parades that first weekend then caught night parades when Wendy or a sitter could watch the girls.

Taking Vanessa home one night and knowing he shouldn't, Scott accompanied her inside to get a drink. He was aroused, a familiar symptom of when he was near Nessa. But it was worse because he had been watching her raise her hands for those silly trinkets and beads. The movement made the sweater she was wearing cling to her breasts. And those pants, they should be burned. Scott had never thought corduroy could be so sexy, but on Nessa it made him crazy. They had to be two sizes too small, and those buttons down the front were too tempting.

Taking the ice cube tray out of her hands, Scott led her to the sofa. He pulled her onto his lap, and kissed her, a soft light caress. He gently held her waist and moved her from one side of his lap to the other making her aware of his arousal. In a husky whisper he said, "This is what you do to me, Nessa."

"If you only knew what you do to me."

He kissed her again, his hand moving inside her sweater. Needing to touch her, Scott reached back to remove Nessa's bra, a skimpy barrier that was too much for him to handle right now. His clumsy fingers couldn't release the clasp, so Vanessa accommodated him by removing it herself.

Vanessa was shocked at her own daring, but was bolstered by what she saw in his eyes, that same dark, intense gaze that was becoming so familiar to her, that she pulled her sweater off, baring herself to him.

Never having revealed herself to any man in any way, Vanessa was very nervous but also very excited. Scott excited her. The idea of touching him excited her, and since Scott was only staring, she did exactly what she'd been wanting to do.

As he watched mesmerized, Vanessa opened his denim shirt button by button and slowly peeled it away. She began tracing her hands along his chest, arms—every exposed part of him.

Feeling her hands on him was electrifying. Needing to return the pleasure, Scott traced her nipples feeling their texture and loving the contrast in color of her dark brown peaks and his hand. He cupped her breast and gently squeezed.

Vanessa gasped. This was new, this was wonderful, this was Scott. He stroked, caressed. When she thought she couldn't take anymore, she felt his hot breath and then his lips on her breast.

Nessa, never having been so aroused before, could feel the tension building up in her. She slowly opened her legs, waiting for and expecting more. Feeling Scott fumbling with the buttons on her pants made her realize just what she was silently asking for. She knew they must stop. She was not ready to help him take her pants off, no matter how tempting the idea was. She carefully stood, put on her sweater, and went into the kitchen to finish making drinks, wishing she had something stronger than soft drinks— stronger then the lingering effects of what Scott made her feel.

Buttoning his shirt, Scott followed her into the kitchen. He had no doubt that she enjoyed their lovemaking as much as he did. He did have doubts about any other feelings she might be having at this moment. He couldn't help himself. He was in love, and he knew that keeping his hands off her was next to impossible. Standing behind her, he rubbed her shoulders in a light caress as she fought with the ice cube tray. He thought a little humor might help to relieve the tension he could feel in her shoulders. "I think we might need a few of those to help cool us off."

"I agree." Feeling another round of shivers race down her spine, Vanessa realized her desire for something stronger to drink would only make Scott's effect on her more intoxicating. Keeping the tray of ice between them as protection, she turned around and found herself willingly trapped in his embrace, the heat of Scott in front of her, the hardness of the counter behind her, and a cold wet tray of ice between them. "The other one melted while we were...busy," she quietly answered.

"And if we're not careful we might start these boiling. You are so beautiful, Nessa, and wonderful, and I'm in awe of how good we are together. In every way," he added.

"But we've only been dating for such a short time—a month. That's only four weeks, twenty-eight days."

"Yep, about six hundred seventy-two hours. I know, teach." He smiled. "Should I go into minutes and seconds?" Unable to keep his love or his hands to himself anymore, Scott pulled her close again. "I love you, Nessa." Then looking into her eyes he asked, "Marry me, please?"

Not expecting anything like this, she dropped the ice cube tray and jumped into his arms. "I love you too, Scott! I just can't believe how quick and easy it was to fall in love with you. And your daughters are wonderful! I love them, too, you know."

"Does that mean yes?"

Realizing she was talking too much, Vanessa nodded her head up and down.

"Soon, Nessa. How soon?"

"In the summer, after school ends."

"That's too long. I'm going to explode before then." He took a deep breath to calm himself. Then he promised, "But for you I'll wait. I can tell that you haven't had much experience, not that I'm complaining. I just want you to know that I plan on making love to you so slow and so long that you'll never want to stop."

"I believe you." Vanessa took his hand and guided him around the melted ice cube puddles and outside to sit on a pair of matching patio chairs. She needed fresh air. They both did.

Facing him and holding both his hands Vanessa said, "You're right, I'm not experienced. As a matter of fact, I'm about as inexperienced as they come."

Scott stared at her. Then a grin appeared on his face. "You mean you're a virgin?"

"Yes, that's what I mean. And take that grin off your face. You look too smug for your own good."

"I'm pleased. It's a pleasant surprise. Let's say I'm proud to have the privilege of being your one and only. I am going to be your only, right?"

"Of course. You are the first man ever to touch me. The first man I ever wanted to touch me."

"But you're so beautiful, Nessa. I mean, no one's ever tried to…"

"They've tried, but I've always resisted. It was easy. They weren't you," Vanessa confessed. "I was waiting for you, and I'm glad you're willing to do the same for me. I know it's going to be hard because I have been trying to control myself from the moment I set eyes on you. But, you see, I want our wedding night to be special, and since I've waited all this time, a few more months shouldn't kill either of us. We can handle it."

Scott wasn't too sure about his self-control, but he was willing to try. He reached for Nessa and settled her onto his lap again. "Nessa, I have no problem with waiting. Well, maybe a slight problem. I can't promise that I'll never touch you again, that experience is too pleasurable. You can see what happened to my promise to take things slow in this relationship. I can't help it. I love touching you, and being touched by you. That way we can still experience many pleasures together. You do realize that since numbers are never ending that means there are an infinite amount of pleasures we can still indulge in." As he spoke, Scott traced her collar bone and moved down to cover her breast with the palm of his hand. Feeling her nipple harden in response he pulled back, saying, "With such a wide variety of pleasures I can't possibly promise to keep my hands to myself But I won't let my desire get out of hand."

Trusting him and wanting to experience those wonderful feelings again, Vanessa nodded and sealed the agreement with a kiss.

"I'd better go," Scott moaned. "Got any of those ice cubes left? If I put a few in my pants I might be able to go to sleep tonight."

"Scott, I love you. Now go home."

Hugging her once more and turning her in the direction of her apartment door Scott commanded, "Nessa, I love you. Now go inside. And make some wedding plans. I'll be working on the honeymoon myself."

CHAPTER FOURTEEN

It was Saturday evening and Vanessa still couldn't believe that she was going to a Mardi Gras ball. She didn't even remember the name of the club, but she was excited about going. Scott had casually asked if she wanted to go. What a crazy question! Of course she wanted to go. His boss, a member of the parade krewe, had invited other members of the architecture firm to attend. Vanessa had never been to a Mardi Gras ball before. Not even one for Zulu or Nomtoc, the predominantly black organizations.

Vanessa called on Monica for help. They went on a shopping spree to find the perfect gown. This was the first time she would choose and dress just for a date with Scott. The gown had a V-shaped bodice just like the navy cocktail dress she'd worn when they had gone to see a play, but this dress was a full-length black chiffon creation. It had thin spaghetti straps that crossed in front, drawing attention to her breasts, then circled her neck to form a halter. It left her back exposed, a bit daring for her, but she couldn't pass it up. There was a matching jacket. Not much of a jacket, really, but it was beautiful. It too was black with strands of gold woven into the lightweight material. A matching purse and high-heeled shoes completed the outfit.

Fully dressed and waiting for Scott, her fiancé, Vanessa couldn't keep still. Getting used to the idea of having a fiancé, Vanessa said the word again to herself, liking the sound. Their engagement was unofficially official. They'd decided to savor it for themselves for a while. After all, Scott hadn't met all of her family yet.

Stopping to admire herself in the full-length mirror, she decided to put the jacket on. If Scott saw her with that much skin exposed he might demonstrate another of those pleasures they'd been enjoying lately. She knew he'd keep the promise he had made two days ago, but the thought of him undressing her was too tempting.

The doorbell rang as she finished adjusting the jacket. Vanessa opened the door and was stunned to see how handsome he looked in a tuxedo. Scott was gorgeous, in a tux, in sweats, and even in jeans that smelled like baby powder. She wanted to pull his clothes off, and ask him to forget about the ball, forget about promises, and make love! But calming herself, Vanessa made do with a kiss.

"Nessa, you'd better get us out of here now. You...are...so...beautiful!"

"And you look twice as good to me. So we'd better get going before we eat each other up," she said guiding him out the door.

Scott divided his attention between Nessa and the street as he drove. He caressed her cheek, her neck, and her ears— anything he could reach. Making it safely to their destination, he parked, turned off the lights, and reached for her. With gentle fingers he grazed her ears as he drew her close to match the kiss she'd given him earlier.

Vanessa considered it a beautiful start of a beautiful night. Walking into the ballroom fifteen minutes later with Scott was a wonderful experience. He introduced her to his boss who was dressed as a duke and a few co-workers she had not met. Vanessa was surprised to hear remarks like: "So, this is Nessa," or, "I'm glad to finally come face to face with you," and even, "It's great to finally meet you, now put this man out of his misery and marry him."

She had just met these people, but they obviously knew a lot about her. She looked at Scott questioningly.

He sheepishly admitted, "I guess I talk too much, but I couldn't help myself. Let's dance."

As Scott pulled her onto the dance floor Vanessa noticed a costumed member of the krewe join the crowd they'd just left. He muttered just loud enough for her to hear, "My God, Scott can't be serious about that woman!"

Vanessa turned to Scott wondering if he'd heard the comment. He seemed a bit preoccupied and only smiled and pulled her close for the slow song that had just begun. Vanessa was glad he hadn't heard after all. She was pleased to see the man get some nasty looks from the people surrounding him. It helped her to ignore the remark and concentrate on Scott and having a good time.

Scott and Vanessa danced, ate, and socialized, unaware of the unreasonable hatred directed at them as a couple. Vanessa was enjoying the feel of Scott's hands on her back. She felt warm, safe, and loved.

They watched the presentation of the krewe members in their beautiful costumes. Tiring of the crowd and being far more interested in each other, Scott and Vanessa decided to sneak away early. They went to her apartment with thoughts of indulging in some of those pleasures Scott mentioned before. When they got there, Scott helped Vanessa unzip her gown. The zipper wasn't difficult for her to reach, but this night...this night, she was feeling bold. Scott appeared in her bedroom door exactly ten seconds after she'd left him standing in the middle of her living room. "After holding you all night and finally getting to unzip that gown, you didn't think I'd be able to stay away from pleasure number fifty-eight?"

"Pleasure number fifty-eight? Have we gotten that far? I need to keep track."

"Pleasure number fifty-eight, watching you undress."

Scott had taken his coat off and rolled up his sleeves. He looked even more gorgeous than before, more relaxed except for the hot, intense gaze in his eyes.

Vanessa slowly let the thin straps fall off each shoulder, slipping one arm through at a time. As she turned to him the chiffon slid down her body to billow at her feet. She proudly stood before him wearing only her one-piece black teddy. It was strapless and molded to her body like nothing Scott had ever seen before.

Scott didn't touch her. He couldn't and still keep his promise. She's a virgin, he reminded himself and, pleasure fifty-eight was too much for him.

"I'll be waiting outside. Maybe we can take a ride or something?" he suggested, hurrying out the door.

Scott grabbed the jacket to his tux and paced up and down Vanessa's driveway as he waited for her to change. Pleasure number fifty-eight left him too frustrated. He didn't want to leave her yet. The night wasn't over, and he had some unfinished business to attend to.

They decided to drive to the lake. The same place, Scott remembered, that Nessa had confessed to making a wish on a star. A wish to find him again. And it came true. Scott hoped it would work for him too.

The lake was a public place, but they found a little corner that was deserted because of the late hour. Scott was looking for privacy, but also space. Her apartment was too closed in, too intimate for his good intentions. And a man could only take so much.

They sat in the car, a light breeze blowing through the window. Now that he could trust himself to touch her, Scott held her hands as they made wedding plans, a safe topic. He'd make sure they steered away from discussing the honeymoon just now.

"I've always wanted a small wedding," Vanessa said. "Nothing too big. What do you think, Scott?"

"How small are you talking about?" he asked, ready to delve into the subject. "Let's see, what are the essentials? It might be important to let the priest come. Then we'd need some witnesses. And I don't want to have to deal with Vicki and Megan when they find out we got married without them. Not to mention Wendy and your family. They'd all want to kill me for marrying you without even meeting them."

Vanessa laughed. "I only meant that I wanted a small wedding, family and a few friends." She'd noticed a slight change in his voice when he mentioned her family.

"Do you want me to meet your family?" he asked.

"Of course, I'm just not sure you're ready to deal with the whole gang."

"Why? There's something you're not telling me. Let me guess." He cocked a brow. "The rest of you're family is white. No, I met your parents. It must be something else. What secrets are you hiding from me, Nessa?"

"I don't have any family secrets, it's just that..." her voice trailed off.

This was a sore spot for him because he was a little hurt that she seemed so reluctant to introduce him to the rest of her family.

"Are you ashamed of me?"

"Of course not!" Vanessa answered, surprised that he'd even think such a thing. "You've met my parents, and Monica and her kids."

"A select few." A thought suddenly occurred to him. "Are any other members of your family causing you problems?"

"Problems?"

"Yes, in the not so distant past you had a problem even thinking about going out with me. Would the other members of your family have a strong aversion to your marrying a white guy?"

"Oh, no, Scott, they don't care what you look like. As a matter of fact, they all know you're white. It's not a secret. It's just something else to tease and torment me with."

"Why?" he asked, not content with her explanation.

"Let's just say my track record of showing interest in anyone has been zero. I had always let it be known that I wasn't interested in anyone. They'd say, and I quote, 'Nobody was good enough for Ness.' Then you came along, following me around, and almost announcing to the whole church that I was interested in you."

"Did I really do that?"

"It seemed that way to them. It was enough to start their tongues wagging. And of course I had to be different and fall in love with a white guy. It was all just too much. I didn't want to scare you away." She added quietly, "My family can be a bit overwhelming."

"So when do I meet them?"

"Sunday, if you're ready."

"I'm ready for anything," he assured her. "And by the way I am a grown man, you don't have to protect me."

"I know that, but…just wait and see."

After a moment of silence Scott asked, "Are you sure about not having a big wedding? I wouldn't mind, if that's what you want."

"Was your first wedding big?"

"Very," Scott said with a laugh. "It was enormous. Kathy was an only child."

"Tell me about her. Please," Vanessa added when he didn't reply immediately.

Scott was silent for so long that Vanessa thought he wouldn't grant her request.

Finally, he said quietly, "She was like you in almost every way, yet she was different from you in every way."

"What a statement!" Vanessa waited for him to say more. When he remained quiet, she said, "Okay, Scott, what do you mean by that?"

"Well, maybe I said that wrong. I didn't fall in love with you because of the ways you're like Kathy. It's because of all the things that make you, you. Kathy was sweet, loved kids, and was a terrific mother. You're sweet, love kids, and will be a terrific mother to my girls and any other children we may have. But that's where it ends. In every other way you're different. From the color of your skin to the curves I love to trace." He showed his appreciation for her curves by tracing a finger down her shoulder, along the swell of her breast, past her hips, and back up again to tilt her face.

He continued as he held her chin. "And it isn't just your appearance that I fell in love with, although that was a good beginning. You have a sense of adventure and fun that's contagious. You make a regular outing exciting. You make me love to be alive and glad to be a part of your life. I love you, Nessa."

Digging into his pocket, Scott pulled out a black velvet-covered box. "To make it official, I'll ask again. Please be a permanent part of my life. Nessa, marry me." Scott flipped open the box to reveal a heart-shaped diamond solitaire.

For a moment she couldn't say a word. The street lamp above reflected light onto the ring and into her eyes. It seemed to twinkle like a star. Her wish was still coming true. At the same place where it was first made one month ago. Smiling, she said, "Of course I'll marry you. It's fate."

CHAPTER FIFTEEN

Having become officially engaged, Vanessa was bursting with the need to tell someone. That night she called Monica despite the late hour. And they talked for a while. Monica was happy for her sister because she understood the kind of love that existed between Scott and Vanessa. She was the only member of the family, other than their parents, who had seen them together. That was all it took.

"Vanessa," she said, "I think this might be a good time for the gang to meet Scott."

"I know, and Scott wants to meet them all. I hope he still wants to marry me after meeting those crazy people we call family. I'll see you tomorrow."

"G'night Ness, and I know you're excited, but try to go to sleep."

"I'll try," Vanessa said as she hung up.

Vanessa had no need to worry. When Scott accompanied her on Sunday, he fit right in with the Lewis family. He took the teasing well, and even laughed when her nieces made up a song and called it the Vanilla Man song. Vanessa could have died of embarrassment, but Scott just smiled that special smile that showed his dimple and said, "I like your family, Nessa."

Vicki and Megan had a great time playing with all the kids. Of course Jasmine, Tony and Mark claimed them and showed them around.

After the wonderful meal of gumbo and roast with all the trimmings, Vanessa's dad sat next to Scott and demanded, "Well, Scott, what are your intentions toward my baby girl? She doesn't stick with any one guy, and I want to know what you've got planned."

Hitting her with that smile again as his way of asking permission, Scott answered, "Well, Mr. Lewis, I've asked her to marry me."

He got no further. The ring on her left hand, which had gone unnoticed, was spotted first by her mother, then her father, and then it seemed by everyone else.

"Oh Ness!" Joyce said.

"And she said yes!" Calvin bellowed. "That's mighty quick!" He'd gone from demanding to know Scott's intentions to being outraged now that he'd discovered them. "I had a feeling I was going to lose my baby girl to you, but not this fast," he told Scott.

Everyone was looking at the ring and congratulating Scott and Vanessa, completely ignoring Calvin's outburst. After the noise died down, the children went out to play again, and Vanessa's mom, sisters, and sisters-in-law surrounded her. While they discussed wedding plans, Vanessa's brothers drew Scott out to the front porch. Vanessa hadn't realized they were gone until nearly half an hour later.

She jumped up. "Oh no! They've got him. I'd hoped to warn him before they got to him, poor Scott."

"Don't worry, Ness, they won't kill him," Tracy reassured her. "After all, James survived." James was her husband of four years.

"Yeah, but it's been so long since they've done this that they might go overboard."

What they were referring to was the pre-wedding inquisition her brothers and brothers-in-law put a fiancé through. And not one of the women really knew what went on.

Five minutes later, all the men came in.

Rushing over to Scott and checking for bruises, Vanessa apologized. "I'm sorry, I should have warned you about the Inquisition." Finding a smile on his face, Vanessa added, "I see I was worried for nothing."

Scott hugged her. "That's right, you have some great brothers."

"I like this guy," her oldest brother Randy said.

"Yeah, he's cool," Josh added.

"And you have our permission to marry him," John announced. Since this was the twins' first and probably only shot at participating in an inquisition, Josh and John made sure they got their comments in loud and clear—as if Vanessa really needed their permission. She was just glad they liked Scott. It meant a lot to her. And she was relieved that Josh didn't act on his promise to embarrass her by acting outrageous.

No matter how much Nessa begged, Scott refused to reveal anything that happened outside. He claimed to be sworn to secrecy.

Joyce asked Vanessa and Scott to stay awhile after everyone left. Feeling like a kid and knowing what was coming, Vanessa sat on the sofa with Scott directly across from her parents. Vicki and Megan were occupied with some very important business, coloring a picture for their soon-to-be grandparents.

Without giving her mother a chance, Vanessa started the discussion she knew was to come.

"I know what you're both worried about. First, we've only known each other a short time, but I have it on good authority that there's no time frame on falling in love, and we do love each other."

"And exactly whose authority are we talking about?" her father asked.

"Monica's, if you have to know. Since we won't be getting married until summer, it'll give you a chance to get used to the idea. Second, there's the race issue. We've had an encounter or two to deal with, and I know we can handle anything together. Right, Scott?" She stopped long enough to look at him for assurance and encouragement, then quickly went on. "And lastly, I know I'm marrying a man with a ready-made family, but you both know how much I love kids. And you've met those two sweet little girls who seemed to already know this is their new family. We know what we're getting into. I just hope you're going to be happy for me."

After patiently listening to Vanessa's little speech, Joyce asked, "Did you pick a date yet?"

Vanessa, with her eyes wide and her mouth hanging open, didn't seem to be able to answer that question. So

Scott decided to help her out. "Two minutes after the last day of school, if it were up to me."

Having recovered from her shock Vanessa smiled and then blushed knowing exactly why Scott was so anxious for the wedding to be set as soon as possible. "Probably a week after school ends. Ma, Dad…" Vanessa hesitated. "You don't have any words of wisdom. Anything you want to say?"

"It seems to me…" Calvin answered, repeating the words Joyce made him memorize when she realized just how serious Scott and Vanessa were. How she'd known, Calvin would never find out. He'd just have to get used to it. He glanced at his wife, took a deep breath, and began again. "It seems to me that you know what you're going to be dealing with, and I can't live your life for you. It's your decision." Clearing his throat and adding his own thoughts, Calvin spoke to his youngest daughter. "You're a smart, level-headed person, and I trust your judgement, baby girl. Besides," he said with a wink, pointing to Scott, "I kinda like him. And I heard he passed The Inquisition."

"That I did, sir," Scott announced with a grin, finding that he liked his future father-in-law. Scott could tell he wasn't thrilled about the marriage but was keeping his opinion to himself for the love of his daughter.

Joyce whispered to her daughter, "I wish I knew what went on at this inquisition."

Hoping to get the men to leak some information, Vanessa suggested, "They probably sit around talking about football or something manly like that."

Joyce laughed. "Or maybe they just stare at each other trying to figure out who's 'Mr. Macho.' "

"Or they arm wrestle! And since Scott passed, he must have beaten them all."

"Good try," said Scott, "but you'll never really know. I've been sworn to secrecy." He looked Calvin straight in the eye to show his appreciation for his open attitude, though grudgingly given. "I think we'll be going now. Thank you, sir."

"Since we'll be family we might as well start off right. That'll be Joyce and Cal." Calvin held out his hand, and the men shook.

Hugging her parents, Vanessa told them goodbye.

Vicki and Megan ran into the room waving their pictures for Maw Maw Joyce and Paw Paw Cal. They had already begun to use the names after hearing them all day by the other children. So they hugged their future grandparents goodbye and were carried out the door by Scott and Vanessa.

After everyone was settled in the car and Scott began to drive, Vicki asked, "MaNessa, are you really gonna be my mommie?"

"Yes, sweetie, I'm really going to be your mommie, and Megan's too."

"Thank you, MaNessa! Thank you, Daddy!"

"What are you thanking me for?" Scott asked, peering into the rearview mirror.

"Because you picked the best mommie!"

"I know I did." Scott reached for Nessa's hand.

CHAPTER SIXTEEN

Valentine's Day landed in the middle of the week this year—a Wednesday, six days before Mardi Gras. With the excitement of two holidays coming up, Vanessa's students were really riled up. They displayed their excitement in the worst possible way. They were teasing, hitting, fighting, and just plain wild. And it wasn't just her class. The whole school seemed to have gone crazy. When the three o'clock bell rang Tuesday afternoon, Vanessa quickly dismissed her students and made her way to her Explorer chanting to herself, "Three more days till Mardi Gras break…" As she waved to some of her co-workers Vanessa recognized the frazzled looks on their faces. She wasn't the only one feeling this way.

Vanessa was relieved the day was over. She had to pick up Scott's present at the engraver's. The shop also specialized in wedding invitations and essentials for a successful reception. She planned on dragging Scott there this weekend to make a final selection on the invitations. She'd been there three times already and had pointed the shop out to Scott in passing.

Her main purpose in coming today was to pick up Scott's Valentine present. She'd put a lot of thought into it and finally decided on a gold watch. It was maybe not as fancy as the one she'd seen him wearing, but it was of good quality. She'd chosen the watch because of what it symbolized: time. Not just time as in seconds, minutes, and hours. But their time. It was their time to meet and fall in love. They were drawn together and nearly collided when they

first met. The inscription on the back was a remembrance
of that day. It read:

OUR LOVE WAS A NEAR COLLISION
YOURS ALWAYS, NESSA

Having picked up the watch and paid for the inscription, Vanessa once again looked through the sample of
wedding invitations. She had narrowed it down to two and
was turning to ask a shop assistant about the print options
available when she spotted Scott walking into the shop.
Now, what was he doing here? she wondered. Whatever the
reason she was glad to see him. After such a rough day at
work, she could use a hug. Vanessa was going to do just that
when a thought occurred to her. She conspired with the
shop assistant and convinced her to give a note to Scott.

Vanessa ducked behind a huge ceiling-to-floor framed
picture of a bride and groom toasting their wedding thy.
She peeked around the huge picture to see the giggling
shop assistant hand the note to Scott. He read it and immediately looked her way. The note gave a clue to where he
would find her. He couldn't miss her.

Hidden pleasures await.
Look behind picture #1.
Your Nessa

He saw her and his eyebrows went up. That heated
smoky gaze trapped her.

Maybe this wasn't a good idea. This is a public place,
Vanessa thought. Too late, he was there.

"Are you my hidden pleasure?" Scott asked.

"I think I am," she answered.

"Good." He pulled her into his arms to give her the hug she'd been needing.

"How did you know this is what I needed?" Vanessa sighed.

"Feels good?"

"Yes."

"Not all pleasures are the same, you know."

"Well, I like this one." She sighed again, breathing in the scent of him. "How did you know I needed this?"

"I don't know. Just the look in your eyes. I thought some Scott therapy was in order."

"It was. It is," she corrected, enjoying the moment. She snuggled closer when he tried to pull away. "I'm not finished yet." She hugged him tighter.

"I'm glad I showed up. I can't have you handing out notes and hugging just any man you see."

"Only you. This is Scott therapy, remember?"

The shop assistant came around the side of the picture with a box full of champagne glasses. She stopped short when she saw them. Champagne glasses rattled in the cardboard box. "I'm sorry, I forgot you were there."

"It's okay, we're just leaving," Scott said and followed a red-faced Nessa to the front of the store.

Vanessa found herself giggling. "These pleasures are starting to get us into trouble."

"And you started it this time," he answered, eyeing the package in her hand. "Are you here for a particular reason?"

"Possibly."

"Were you looking at wedding invitations?"

"Possibly."

"Is that something for me you're hiding behind your back?"

"Possibly." Vanessa wasn't giving out any information, he just had to wait until tomorrow.

"My Valentine?" he pressed.

"Possibly." Boy, was he persistent, she thought, not giving him a clue.

"I see I'm not going to get an answer from you today."

"Not a chance. Tomorrow's soon enough. I'll be waiting for you, six o'clock sharp," she reminded.

"I'll be there," he promised.

Vanessa gave him a quick kiss and was turning to go out the door when she thought to ask, "Are you here for a particular reason?"

"Possibly." He grinned.

"Ah-ha, my Valentine present?"

"Possibly."

"I see," she said, "I'll find out tomorrow. And who knows there might by some other hidden pleasures waiting for you."

Scott smiled as he watched her leave the store. What did he start? These pleasures were getting them into trouble. Scott shook his head in wonder pleased that she was enjoying them as much as he did. Tomorrow couldn't get here fast enough.

CHAPTER SEVENTEEN

Having experienced a peaceful Valentine's day at work, Vanessa realized it was only the calm before the storm. There weren't any parties planned, but the children got to exchange Valentines at the end of the day. Because they didn't want to be denied that privilege, they behaved very well all morning.

Unfortunately, the restlessness and rowdiness would return with the excitement of having their own parade around the school on Friday afternoon. Just two more days till Mardi Gras break, then it would all be over because after Mardi Gras her class would turn back to normal. Until Easter. Vanessa hated that restless time before any holiday, but she was finished thinking about school right now. She had plans to spend the evening with her Valentine. First, she had to visit her little Valentines. Scott was still at work, but Vanessa knew Vicki and Megan were home with Laura, the sitter. Since Scott was picking her up later, she wouldn't get to see the girls then, so she decided to stop by on her way home.

Before she had pulled all the way into the driveway, Vanessa could see two little heads peeking through the living room curtain. As she walked to the front door, Vanessa heard, "MaNessa, MaNessa, MaNessa!" and, "Hurry, Miss Laura, hurry!"

When Miss Laura opened the door they literally jumped into Nessa's arms.

Megan kissed Vanessa on the cheek saying, "Happy Balentine, MaNessa!"

"It's V-V-V-Valentine, Megan," Vicki corrected, giving Vanessa a hug. "I told her all day."

"B-B-B-Balentine, Balentine, Balentine!" Megan repeated.

"I think it might be a good idea to keep reminding her," said Nessa, "She'll get it right if we keep trying. Isn't that right?"

"Yes, yes, yes," Megan answered.

"Okay, MaNessa," Vicki said.

"Good. Now guess what? I have a Valentine for both of you because you're my special little girls."

"Did Tony, Mark, and Jasmine get a Valentine, too?" Vicki asked, being loyal to her new friends and future cousins.

"Of course they did. I pretended to be Cupid, and left a surprise on their doorstep. I rang the bell and then ran away."

Vicki giggled.

"And you know what?"

"What?" Vicki asked wide-eyed.

"I think Jasmine saw me. I heard her yell, 'Bye Auntie Cupid!' "

The girls thought that was hilarious. "But I had to bring my Valentine straight to you because I have a special song to go with it."

They hopped onto her lap as Vanessa took out two plastic heart-shaped pink and white pendants, each hanging from silky pink yarn. She opened each one. Inside was a picture. One with Vanessa and Vicki, and one with Vanessa and Megan. They were pictures they'd taken about a week ago in one of those mall photo booths. Vanessa settled both wiggling girls on her lap. As they stared in wonder at the picture she pressed a button in the middle of Megan's pendant. It started a tune. Vanessa sang, "You are my Megan, my only Megan," to the tune of "You Are My Sunshine."

And of course she then pressed the button in the middle of Vicki's heart to start the tune and sang to her too. At the end of the song, Vicki hugged Vanessa again saying, "I love you, MaNessa!"

"Me too!" said Megan, making sure she got a hug in too.

Vanessa's heart swelled. She gave each little cheek a kiss goodbye. "I love you, but it's time for me to go right now. Be good for Miss Laura, and take care of those necklaces."

The girls walked her to the front door and waved their good-byes with Miss Laura smiling on. Vanessa left to the sounds of two happy little girls and the melody of "You Are My Sunshine" still ringing in her ears.

CHAPTER EIGHTEEN

When Scott rang the doorbell Vanessa immediately opened it and pulled him inside, caressing his lips with kisses.

"Happy Valentine's!" she said, handing Scott a box wrapped in shiny red and white striped paper.

"The guy's supposed to say that first," he told her.

"Really!" She smiled. "Is that a law?"

"If it was, it's too late, you already broke it," Scott pointed out.

"Oh, well, then you'll have to open my present first."

Nessa was so eager for him to open the present that it piqued Scott's curiosity. He was anxious to see what was inside.

He unwrapped the red and white paper and lifted the lid of the black box. She didn't give him a chance to get a close look at the watch inside, and not a second to thank her before it was snatched out of his hands.

"Scott, wait, I have to explain before you put it on."

"You mean I get it back! I get to keep it?" he asked, amused at her excitement.

"Of course you get it back. I bought it for you. Just listen a minute."

Scott leaned back onto the sofa. He loved the sound of her voice and could stay here all night listening to her talk. But then that would lead to staring at her mouth and possibly the beginning of some interesting pleasures, which might end up spoiling the plan he'd made for them tonight…

"Scott!"

"Hmmm, what?"

"Are you listening to me?"

"Of course I am," he told her, staring into her eyes instead of at her lips.

"I was saying that I bought you this watch because of what it means to us. You tell time with a watch in seconds, minutes, and hours. But when I think about us and time, I think about the saying, 'There's a time for everything.' "

Scott smiled as he watched her move her hands as she spoke.

"It's true," she insisted. "Don't you believe me?"

"I do. And I agree."

"Good, because now is the time for us. I was waiting for you; we were meant to be. There was no way we were going to miss meeting each other that first day."

"I know, I felt it too," Scott whispered.

"When you wear this watch, I want you to think about me—us—on that first day we met." Vanessa handed the watch back. "There's an inscription."

As she spoke, Scott found himself falling in love with his present and he hadn't even touched it yet. When he turned it over to read the inscription he knew he'd cherish it for the rest of his life. It was about their beginning—their time. That day always brought a smile to his face. It brought Nessa. What more could he ask for?

"Thank you, My Nessa," Scott said with such simple sincerity that Vanessa knew just how deeply he felt. "Pleasure number sixty-five, realizing just how lucky I am."

Vanessa was overjoyed with his reaction. So much so that she was surprised when he produced a long narrow box with a ribbon for her to open.

Flowers? Vanessa thought. She liked flowers. Nessa didn't know too many women who didn't.

She opened the box, and she did find flowers, three red roses. They were wrapped in green tissue and tucked next to three smaller boxes, each separately wrapped: one in gold, another red, and the last one green. When she reached inside to pick up the roses, Scott stopped her with a touch of his hand.

"One at a time." He handed her one red rose and the gold-covered box.

Vanessa unwrapped it and found a small, clear box, with a statue of Cupid inside. She could see another smaller box inside the cube at Cupid's feet. He was holding a shiny gold heart with writing engraved on it. She lifted the lid and took him out, the smaller box falling into her lap and landing next to her rose. The inscription said:

You're in my heart.

Vanessa fell in love with it. If Cupid hadn't already worked on her heart, this would have done it.

"Go on, open it," Scott prompted, taking the small box from her lap and placing it in her hands.

Vanessa put Cupid on the coffee table and opened the other box. Inside was a pair of heart shaped diamond earrings.

"Scott, these are so beautiful."

"And there's more." He handed her another rose, and another box.

She opened the second box. Inside was another Cupid, holding another heart with a box at his feet. Engraved on the heart was another message.

You're in my soul.

Vanessa took a deep breath. This man was so sweet. She looked into his eyes. "You are my heart and soul, Scott."

She opened the smaller box and found a pair of ruby earrings.

"You explained your gift, now let me," he said, moving closer. "When I'm with you, I feel so alive that my soul is glowing from the inside out. This is the color I imagine my soul to be when I'm around you, full of life and fire."

That was so romantic. Vanessa reached over to show him how much she appreciated the gift, and the words. He stopped her with a light caress along the curve of her ear with the third rose. She shivered with longing.

"There's one more."

So there was, she thought. But nothing could be better than the words spoken to her by Scott.

She uncovered the green paper from the last present. She found another Cupid, just as she suspected. He was holding a heart, and had a box at his feet, just like the others. Vanessa took her time taking him out of the box and wondering what words could possibly be there waiting there for her to read.

Scott got her attention with the brush of the rose. "Do you want me to read it to you?"

"No." She smiled. "I'm just savoring the moment."

She held the last Cupid:

You are the music in my life.

Yes, they both loved music. Hearts, souls, music—it all fit together. This last Cupid came with a pair of emerald studs.

"The emeralds remind me of music," Scott quietly told her. "Music creates such a feeling of contentment and completeness inside me. You, my Nessa, are the music in my life."

"Scott, I don't know what to say. This, no, these are the most beautiful presents I've ever gotten."

"No. You were right the first time, it's a present, not presents. It's one present broken up into small parts. Each part shows how important you are to me. Can I read it all to you?"

"Yes, I'd love that," she answered, waiting to hear his husky voice as he spoke the words engraved on the hearts.

You're in my heart.
You're in my soul.
You're the music in my life.

"It's like a song, Scott. It's wonderful. I don't know what else to say."

"Say thank you," he whispered.

"Thank you," she repeated, putting all her love in those two words.

As Scott fastened the diamond earrings into her ears, Vanessa indulged in pleasure number sixty-six. It involved her lips and Scott's ears. She was surprised to find that they had something else in common. Vanessa thought, this night will be unforgettable. And it was, in more ways than one. Scott surprised her with a moonlight cruise down the Mississippi aboard the Natchez, one of New Orleans's very own paddle wheelers. As they waited to board the boat, they bumped into one of Scott's co-workers in line ahead of them.

Vanessa heard the man bragging about his apartment in the newly restored Cotton Mill complex in the historic warehouse district. At one time it had been a warehouse. Vanessa knew that the one hundred-fifteen-year old building had been restored and converted into condominiums and penthouse apartments. It was somewhat pricey and popular with young executives like the one standing in front of them bragging. Vanessa could understand the man being proud of where he lived, but he was going on and on and on. She sighed, feeling sorry for his date as he continued to boast.

"It's beautiful inside and constructed so that there's exclusive access. We don't want just anybody coming in," he told his date. "I could give you a tour, show you the fitness center. And maybe we could work out together," he suggested as if he was doing her a huge favor.

He turned and saw Scott and Vanessa waiting to board the steamboat behind them. He smiled and gave Scott a welcoming pat on the shoulder. As Scott introduced T.J. to her the man's expression suddenly changed, but he quickly recovered himself to paste on a smile for Scott's benefit. That was when she recognized him. This was the boss's son, the same guy who had made that nasty comment at the ball. She'd put it out of her mind and had simply forgotten him, especially since everyone else had been so nice.

He acted pleased to meet her, but remembering his remark that night, Vanessa could tell he didn't mean a word he said. So she figured two could play at that game and pretended to be just as pleased to meet him. Scott didn't seem to notice anything odd.

As T.J. began to board ahead of them, Vanessa saw him nod his head in their direction and whisper something to his date. Vanessa turned her back at his insulting gaze and missed seeing his date deck him in the eye. What she did have the pleasure to witness was the blur of red and white the girl created as she raced past them.

Scott, finally finding the tickets in his wallet, looked up in time to see T.J.'s date and then T.J. himself leaving the area in a big hurry.

"What happened?" he asked Vanessa.

"I'm not exactly sure," Vanessa answered, glad that some people weren't as ignorant. T.J. had gotten what he deserved.

They both watched as T.J. raced after his date. "Melissa, wait a second! It was just a joke, can't you take a joke. You gotta admit he does need glasses!" T.J. stopped at the end of the ramp leading to the paddle wheeler, no longer racing after his date. Instead he shouted, "I guess we both need something to correct our vision. We're both messing around with the wrong kind of woman."

Vanessa grabbed Scott's hand, holding him back. "I think we pretty much know what happened. Let it go."

"But I work with the man…"

"And if you have to, you can deal with him there. Don't worry about him, come be my Valentine."

"I already am."

"Prove it."

"I intend to."

T.J. had long ago faded from Vanessa's thoughts as she enjoyed her evening with Scott. They stood at the rail and gazed at the moonlit sky. They spent the evening talking about everything: where they'd live, Vicki and Megan, names for their future children, New Orleans, their jobs, the parade that went on without them that night, everything.

When they ran out of topics, Scott suggested dinner from the buffet. There was a variety of famous New Orleans dishes: jambalaya, crayfish étouffée, fried shrimp and fish, and seafood gumbo.

For Valentine's, the Natchez was transformed into the Love Boat; the atmosphere of the dining room was made for lovers. Soft music, muted lights, and red votive candles in heart-shaped crystal holders made each pair of diners feel as if they were all alone.

For Vanessa, the best part of the meal was dessert. She found that she enjoyed sharing with Scott as they fed each other pecan pie and bread pudding with rum sauce. She particularly enjoyed Scott's method of cleaning the gooey rum sauce from the pudding off her fingers. Another pleasure.

Vanessa didn't want the night to end. By eleven o'clock they were outside her apartment and tomorrow was only an hour away. Scott had driven her home and walked her to the door to kiss her goodnight. Lingering and not wanting to part, Scott finally broke away and whispered, "Goodnight love."

Yes, this night was unforgettable, Vanessa thought, stepping into her apartment.

CHAPTER NINETEEN

Finally on Mardi Gras break, Vanessa rode out to Scott's house on her bike early Saturday morning with a surprise of donuts and chocolate milk for the girls. She could hear the "Sunshine" song as she stood at the door.

"They must be driving you crazy with that song," she said when Scott opened the door to let her in.

"Of course not."

"No?" she asked not believing him. "Why not?"

"Come see. We've got something to show you," he told her. "Girls, MaNessa's here!"

"Asong, asong, asong," Megan confirmed.

"You sit down on the sofa while we perform for you," Scott told her, standing the girls up on the coffee table. He counted, "One, two, three."

The girls started the tune again on their lockets and began to sing, "You are MaNessa, my only Nessa."

Vanessa smiled. That was so sweet. She was pleased that the girls, from the beginning, had accepted her in their lives so readily. Singing that song to her showed Vanessa that the bond they had was growing stronger every day.

"That was really good," she told them, stretching her arms wide. They jumped and Vanessa caught each for a big hug.

The girls were ready to do a repeat performance so Vanessa took a turn and sang, jazzing up the beat while everybody danced. Next thing she knew, Vicki, Megan, and Scott had joined in the singing. They kept right on singing until they had done the Sunshine song for everyone.

When Vicki suggested they sing for Maw Maw Joyce, Paw Paw Cal, Aunt Monica, Aunt Wendy, Jasmine, Tony, Mark, and all her relatives, Vanessa knew it was time to stop.

"We could go on singing forever if we did that," she told the girls.

"I want to sing fo'ever and ever!" Megan shouted.

Vanessa glanced at Scott. "What do you think?"

"I think," he said, lifting Vicki and then Megan back onto the table, "that this should be our song." He pulled Nessa close. "Our family song."

"I'd like that." She wrapped her arm around his waist. "What do you say, girls?"

"Yes!" Vicki shouted.

"Yes, yes, yes!" Megan echoed.

It was final. Vanessa felt right at home in Scott's house with his kids. No wonder Scott was so comfortable with her family. This spontaneous bonding was so familiar. It was as natural as breathing.

Vanessa poured the girls some chocolate milk and gave each one a donut.

Bringing over two mugs of coffee, Scott joined them at the kitchen table giving Vanessa a kiss on the forehead.

"How about me, Daddy?" Vicki asked, kneeling on her chair. She closed her eyes, leaned forward, and waited for her kiss. The whole time she held her milk in one hand.

"Me, me, me, too!" Megan insisted.

Scott obliged and relaxed when they both sat down without spilling one drop of milk.

Content with the direction her life was taking, Vanessa sat and drank it all in. Sitting here with her own little family, the natural way they did something as simple as having breakfast or singing a silly song together, was so...right. She couldn't stop the smile that began to spread across her face.

Scott had been watching the different expressions move across Nessa's face. She looked content, thoughtful, then downright happy. Hoping she was thinking about him, Scott asked, "What are you smiling about?"

"I'm just happy, one big bowl of sunshine."

"Ah-ah, and you started it!"

"I guess I'm guilty!" She blew her coffee to cool it off. "But whose idea was it to sing to me?"

"I didn't put them up to it. It was all their idea, right girls?" Scott asked.

"It was my idea," Vicki explained. "Megan wanted to do it too."

Scott said, "And last night before they went to bed, they surprised me. Vicki and Megan sang the song to me."

"And we wanted to sing to you, too, MaNessa, but Daddy said to wait." Vicki gave Nessa an anxious look. "And you liked it, didn't you?"

"I loved it!"

"Now, you see why I'm not tired of that song?" Scott asked. "That was a wonderful gift you gave them. Thanks, Nessa."

"You don't have to thank me. They're my girls, too."

"They are, aren't they? We're already a family. We've even got a song." Scott laughed.

Vanessa sighed happily. None of the problems she thought they would have when she first got involved with Scott had materialized. Maybe she had only been looking for trouble. After all, Jessica and Adam were a happily-married couple. Maybe most people weren't as intolerant of differences as she thought, excluding T.J. of course.

Vanessa decided never to doubt her good fortune again.

CHAPTER TWENTY

The next two days passed quickly. Vanessa spent time with the girls, giving Laura a break while Scott was at work, and at night they went to see the parades. Scott and Vanessa soon had aching necks due to two little girls sitting on their shoulders, so Scott decided to make a ladder for them. He bought the materials he needed and they went to work. It was a simple, white wooden seat designed to be secured across the top of the ladder. After it dried, and with Vicki's and Megan's help, Vanessa stenciled in purple, gold, and green hearts, butterflies, and flowers. It looked like Mardi Gras and spring rolled together.

Scott was excited about having a safe place for the girls to watch the parades and still leave the adults pain-free. At least the excuse he used was a good one no doubt. Vanessa knew he saw this as an opportunity to catch more trinkets, but he wouldn't admit it.

Four o'clock Mardi Gras morning Vanessa got a wake-up call. "Nessa, are you still asleep?"

"Yeah," she answered groggily.

"Well, then you have to get up! We have to get a good spot. You won't believe all the people I saw on the news camped out on St. Charles Avenue!"

"I know, I know. I've lived here all my life, remember." She yawned into the phone. "It's too early to get up. We don't normally leave until about eight o'clock."

"You have to be kidding! Most of the good spots are already gone. Look, tell your family to meet us out there. I'll be there to get you in twenty minutes."

Realizing she wasn't going to get this Mardi Gras maniac to see reason, Vanessa reluctantly agreed. This was precisely why she hadn't mentioned that some people camped out the night before.

She quickly washed and got dressed, then got together all the snacks for the picnic they'd have during the parades. She was the snack lady, and Scott was bringing the drinks.

Every Mardi Gras her family joined the thousands of others on St. Charles Avenue to watch the parades and to picnic. It was a family atmosphere, with the exception of a few wild college students, but definitely tame compared to the wild party in the Quarter. She wouldn't dream of entering the French Quarter on Mardi Gras Day with the children.

She picked up the phone to call her sister. Monica was the official chicken fryer; Vanessa knew she'd be getting up soon anyway.

"Hey, Monica, it's me."

"Ness, what are you doing up so early?"

"Scott woke me. He will be here in ten minutes to pick me up. He's got it into his head that we have to leave now to find a spot for the parades."

"Is he nuts?" Monica paused. "Are you nuts?"

"I tried to tell him but he saw all those people camped out on the news. I think he'll go crazy if we don't leave early enough to rope off a good spot. So, just look for us between General Taylor and Napoleon, okay."

"Okay, Ness," Monica laughed. "Girl, I can tell you're in love. To wake up at this time of morning to find a good spot, unbelievable," she teased.

Vanessa could imagine Monica shaking her head in wonder on the other end of the phone line. "I know, I know!" was all she could say. She hung up to the sound of Monica's laughter.

Still not believing she was going along with this idea of Scott's to leave her house before the sun had even come up, Vanessa decided to show him exactly how nuts she thought he was. As soon as she saw Scott's headlights, Vanessa grabbed the picnic basket and raced down the driveway to meet him. She jumped into the front seat. "I was ready and waiting for you. And you know, if we had thought about it, you could have blown your horn when you were a block away. That way you wouldn't have had to stop at all. It would have been no problem to throw the basket through the window, keep pace with the car, and jump in right behind it. Then we would probably have saved a few seconds, and that would get us an even better spot for the parades," she teased, a grin splitting her face.

He chuckled as he watched her put the basket on the floor in the back and then get settled in the passenger seat. "Did I really sound that crazy?"

"To a woman who doesn't normally wake up at four in the morning, yes!"

"But you still love me, right?"

"Which is lucky for you!" she admitted.

"Good, at least someone does. Wendy nearly chewed my head off when I called this morning. She said she'd see me when she saw me."

As they drove on she peeked into the back seat again, glad to find Vicki and Megan still sound asleep. They looked cute in their little ballerina outfits.

"What time did you wake up anyway?"

"At about three, I woke up wishing you were with me. I was in the mood for indulging in some of those pleasures you keep promising me."

"I have?" she asked, knowing that he was just trying to charm her into a good mood.

"Yes, you have, but poor me, you weren't anywhere around. So I figured if I had to suffer, I might as well put on the TV. You know, to take my mind off of things."

Vanessa laughed. Scott made it hard to stay mad at him. "Did it work?" she asked.

"Not really, but that's when I put the news on. Lucky for me, huh?"

"I don't think you should ask me that question right now," Vanessa informed him.

They got a good parking space less than a block off St. Charles Avenue. Nessa took the sleeping girls and laid them on top of a few blankets in a big red wagon Scott had somehow stuffed into the trunk along with the ladder and an ice chest. They weren't the only people up and about. Others were unloading cars, picking choice spots, and roping them off.

Scott and Vanessa walked for about a block and a half before they found a large empty spot with an unobstructed view. Scott went back for the chairs and cooler while Vanessa laid the girls on a blanket. They were still sound asleep. Good! The girls waking up right now and wanting to eat, drink, and play would be worse than waking up at four-thirty in the morning to begin with. Vanessa didn't know what she would do to entertain them. She had a few tricks up her sleeve, but it would be hours before everyone else got here. And after that, still a few more hours before the parades started.

Scott returned with chairs and other things from the car. Vanessa put a finger to her lips, signaling Scott to be quiet.

"Okay," he mouthed as he carefully put everything down. While he did this, Vanessa noticed his eyebrows lift, and up popped his dimples.

What was he up to, she wondered. A moment later, Scott pulled her into his arms and nibbled at her ear.

"Scott, what are you doing?"

"Shhh," he whispered, "you'll wake the girls." He moved to her other ear. Vanessa closed her eyes to better enjoy the pleasure. They popped open when she heard a sound coming from the blanket where the girls lay. Her eyeballs moved to peek at them. Megan had turned over, but they were still sleeping.

"Scott."

"Shhhh," he told her again, his lips moving against hers. "You'll wake Vicki and Megan."

Whether or not they were awake was the last thing on her mind now. Vanessa enjoyed his kisses until she heard a muffled curse and a loud crash. Remembering that they were in the open and in a public place, Vanessa pulled away from Scott. "I should have known by the look in your eye that you were up to no good."

"No good? That was very good. I enjoyed pleasure number seventy eight, getting my fiancée all hot and bothered without anyone noticing and without waking the girls."

"The girls! They're still asleep?" She walked over to them. "Thank God! No more public pleasures, Scott Halloway!" she demanded.

"If you insist, my Nessa. That pleasure had its drawbacks anyway."

"It did?"

"It left me all hot and bothered."

She laughed, "Well, it's your own fault."

The things you do to me, Nessa, Scott thought as he went to set up the cooler, folding chairs, and wagon. With the help of some rope he was able to reserve their spot. "What now?" he asked.

"We sit back, relax, and wait." Vanessa sat on the ground and leaned against the cooler. She took out her radio, put on a soft, quiet station, patted a place in front of her, and waited for Scott to join her.

This was a safe pleasure, he thought. There was something special about quietly watching the sun come up while a beautiful woman played with your hair. Yes, this is nice, he repeated to himself as he fell asleep. Pleasure number seventy-nine.

Vanessa heard him snore softly. His whole body was relaxed against her. She watched as his chest moved with each breath he took and couldn't resist unbuttoning the two buttons on his purple, gold and green pull over shirt. She placed her hand over his heart, enjoying the strong even beat. She liked the feel of his chest hairs as they curled around her fingers.

But enough of that, she decided. This wasn't the time or the place. Besides, it was more enjoyable when he was awake. She brushed her hand across his chest one last time and sighed.

At least I know his snoring doesn't bother me, she thought, wondering what she was going to do now that they were settled and everyone else was sleeping. She wasn't the least bit tired.

She remembered the mystery in her purse and was glad she'd brought it along. When she was reading, time always flew by.

Just as she read the last sentence and closed the book, Monica, her parents, and the whole gang began to appear.

"Well, what have we here?" Josh teased. "And exactly how early were you up to get this great spot?"

"I'm sure you already know," Vanessa grumbled as she tried to get the kinks out of her neck.

"Leave her alone, Josh," Monica laughingly defended. "Ness took pity on you and tried to come a little early."

"Hey, Auntie Ness!" Jasmine, Tony, and Mark yelled at the head of the gang closing in on them.

"Hi guys," she answered. To Monica she said, "We've just been lying around."

"So I see." Not bothering to hide her smile, her mother looking at the comfortable position Scott still held. He was starting to move.

"Hey everybody." Scott stretched. "I didn't know I was that tired. How long did I sleep, Nessa?"

"About three hours."

"It's eight o'clock already!" As he got up, Scott realized, "And I slept on you the whole time! I'm sorry, you should have woken me."

"I was reading, so I didn't feel it at the time."

"Let me help you up," he insisted, rubbing her lower back. Vanessa got up stiffly and was a little embarrassed at having her family witness what she considered a private moment, which was kind of silly after the early morning show they had put on for everyone who was out this morning. She hadn't believed Scott's claim that no one saw them even though it was still a little dark at the time.

"It's okay, Nessa," Scott whispered, "I'm only trying to get the kinks out. No more public pleasures, I promise."

"Will you stop staring," her father demanded. "You'd think you never saw a man show some concern for his fiancée before. And bring out that fruit and those donuts. These kids are gonna want something to eat."

As they filed in, everyone else came over and congratulated Scott and Vanessa on picking such a good spot. They were normally behind a large group with all the best spots already taken.

John suggested, "Why don't you two reserve us a spot every year!"

"See what you started," Vanessa said, turning and poking a finger into Scott's chest. But she wasn't mad. How could she be mad when he was still giving her such a wonderful back rub.

"I don't mind, as long as you're there to be my pillow every year," he whispered into her ear, sending tingles down her spine.

"Daddy, Daddy, Daddy! Go potty," a tiny voice demanded.

"Me too, Daddy," added Vicki.

"Oh-oh," Scott murmured as he looked around. "Where do you go potty here!"

"You mean I haven't told you about that little joy of Mardi Gras? Port-O-Lets," Vanessa slowly stated.

"Oh, no!" Scott moaned.

"Oh, yes!" Vanessa laughed.

Despite being forced to use the portable toilets positioned all along the parade route, Mardi Gras was a lot of fun. The kids took turns in the ladder and caught tons of beads and trinkets. And Wendy, Jack, and the boys did show up sometime before ten that morning. They watched the Zulu, Rex, and Truck parades. They also ate, drank, and had an all-around good time. It was a tired crew that made their way back to their cars as the last truck float went by.

CHAPTER TWENTY-ONE

As the weather turned warmer, Scott, Vanessa, Vicki, and Megan spent a lot of time in the bright sunshine. They flew kites and rode bikes with the girls, who jealously made certain that each had a turn riding with Vanessa.

Sometimes when they fed the ducks, a smile passed between Scott and Vanessa at the memory of the first time they had done that together. Spotting old ladies, or simply enjoying the shade of a huge oak tree at the park had them cracking up with laughter. Picnicking at City Park or Bayou St. John was another one of their favorite pastimes. And of course there was movie night with the Jones clan. Vicki and Megan loved the idea of having new cousins, especially since Tony, Mark and Jasmine were among them.

They continued going to church and visiting her parents every Sunday and were already considered a family unit to Vanessa's family, not to mention Scott's. On one occasion Wendy, Jack, and their two boys joined them after church. Wendy was happy for her little brother and already considered Vanessa her sister-in-law. She took credit for their meeting when she found out everything that happened that first day. "After all," Wendy insisted, "if I hadn't sent Dee-Dee after Scott, he'd have never hid out by going to Storyland and would have never seen Vanessa again. And who was it that dragged Scott to church?" she demanded.

Scott knew it was no use arguing, so he let Wendy take all the credit. But he was positive there were other forces involved. He glanced at the watch Nessa had given him. It was the only one he wore. It had been their time. If they hadn't met that day, it would have happened not long after.

Sometimes Scott had extra work from the new design for a hotel project his firm was working on near Canal Street. Vanessa would come over to help keep the girls busy. They'd order pizza or she'd cook something with a lot of extra help from Vicki and Megan. Afterward, they'd wash and put the girls to bed together. They'd snuggle on the sofa for an hour or so, listening to oldies and tempting each other with pleasures. But as promised, Scott always controlled himself, escorted Nessa to her car, kissed her senseless, and tried to get back to work. He couldn't wait for the day when home for Nessa would be with him. Vanessa felt the same and was relieved that Scott was the one with all the self-control.

Sometimes Scott was there to give her a helping hand, too. On one particularly sunny day Vanessa left school with the ringing of the bell. She had tons of work to correct and knew there was no way she'd get anything done cooped up in her classroom. She stuffed her official Looney Toons teacher's bag full of reading, math, and spelling tests.

To help make this chore more festive, Vanessa created a picnic atmosphere in her little backyard. She settled down with a blanket, a huge cup of iced tea, and a bowl of popcorn. The part of teaching she liked was the interaction with her students, making them want to learn—that was the easy part. This was boring and tiring, but it had to be done. So putting aside her negative feelings on the matter, Vanessa got down to business.

After correcting and recording two sets of spelling tests and a set of math tests, Vanessa dug in her bag for another set of tests. Suddenly she felt a kiss on her neck. She was facing her neighbor's backyard, so she hadn't seen or heard anyone come in. But there was no mistaking the identity of those lips, especially when they made their way to her ear.

The stack of papers was forgotten as Vanessa rolled over, then straddled his hips and gave him back just what he deserved—the sweetest kisses she could return. Unfortunately they were interrupted. By Scott himself.

"Nessa," he pleaded.

"What, Scott? I'm not finished yet."

"Yeah, I can tell—but we've got an audience."

That was all it took for awareness to return—awareness of her.

"Oh, hi Sabrina!" Vanessa said, rolling off Scott and trying to compose herself. What an example to set for a teenager with runaway hormones.

Sabrina stared at her with wide brown eyes, obviously not believing what she'd seen; after all this was Miss Vanessa. "I've seen scenes like this in movies, but man!"

"Can we help you, Sabrina?" Scott asked, having mercy on Vanessa who was deeply embarrassed and blushing all over. He remembered meeting Nessa's little neighbor and her attempts to get Vanessa's twin brothers to notice her. He knew Nessa liked Sabrina and wouldn't want to encourage any explicit behavior by setting a bad example.

"Sabina?" Scott asked again when she just stood there, staring at them both.

"Oh, yeah, Mr. Scott. Umm—here's your change, Miss Vanessa. It's from those raffle tickets you bought yesterday."

"Thanks." Vanessa quickly stepped to the fence to get the change. She didn't want Sabrina hopping over and making comments that would definitely cause her even more embarrassment.

"Bye, I'll leave you two alone now," she sighed. "I just wish John or Josh would let me kiss them like that," she muttered, heading toward her back door.

"I see what you mean about Sabrina," Scott said, standing behind Vanessa and pulling her against him.

"Yeah, she's got such a huge crush on my little brothers. I just hope she gives up soon."

"She will eventually."

"Hm-mm." Vanessa squeezed his arms more tightly around her. "And she's always here with one fund raiser or another. Maybe when she grows out of it, she'll stop coming over so often trying to catch them here. It'll certainly keep more money in my pockets."

"Now that's a thought. Feeling better?" he asked. "Are you back to normal?"

"Normal?"

"What I'm asking, my Nessa, is if you're still red all over under that toasty shade of brown I love so much?"

"You know I get embarrassed, just like that," she said snapping her fingers. Turning around to face him she asked, "So why did you sneak up on me like that anyway?"

"Me? I only gave you a few kisses, and before I could blink, I was jumped."

"And you know what made me do that!"

"What?" he asked innocently.

"The ear thing. It turns me into a maniac."

"Okay, I can deal with being attacked once in awhile," he said gravely. He waited for and watched the smile he knew would come when he teased her. Satisfied, Scott asked, "So, what were you doing?"

She made a face. "Checking papers."

"Oh, your favorite pastime."

Scott knew how much she hated grading papers, so he offered, "Mind if I help?"

"Of course not! Wait, let me get another purple pen. Don't change your mind!"

That was just like Nessa, Scott thought. Checking papers with a purple pen. She probably thought of red as the enemy. Most teachers graded in red. But his Nessa was different.

Scott had taken the day off from work. After putting in all those extra hours on the design for the new hotel, he needed a break. He had spent the day hanging around, and going to see a movie. The only thing missing from his day of relaxation was Nessa. He had gone by her school after three o'clock dismissal, but she was already gone. He was glad he had caught up with her, and sneaked a kiss and, he admitted to himself, made her go wild. He savored the knowledge of the power he had to do that to her.

He wondered what would have happened if they weren't interrupted by Sabrina the nosey.

He grinned as Nessa returned with a glass of iced tea for him and another purple pen. "I never thought I'd be looking forward to grading papers," he said, remembering one of his favorite songs. "The things we do for love…"

CHAPTER TWENTY-TWO

Easter came and went. Nessa dragged everyone to the mall to take bunny pictures and buy matching outfits to wear on Easter Sunday. The Easter Bunny was generous with the candy for Vicki and Megan. But he also left a new toothbrush for each as a reminder to brush. Vanessa found an Easter Basket at Scott's house with a white negligee in it. Blushing, she offered to model for Scott but took back the offer when she saw the lustful look in his eyes. Scratch that pleasure.

She had given Scott a basket too. Among an assortment of Easter goodies, he found a pair of silk boxers. These were both practical and fun because from every angle you could spot Bugs and Daffy sprinting across the shorts. Scott promised to model them on their wedding night. Vanessa laughed at the picture of Scott in those shorts, and her in the filmy white gown.

Wedding plans were being made with the help of her mother and sisters. Vanessa was very excited, but still planned to keep it small. Her family, as large as it was, would probably fill most of the small church so the guest list was kept to a minimum. Scott had a few people he wanted to invite, but his list was short when compared to Vanessa's.

They would use the church hall for the reception and decided to let a highly recommended caterer handle the buffet after the ceremony. There would be plenty of food, a necessity at any New Orleans celebration. Vanessa felt she was coping with the wedding plans pretty well. She knew whatever Scott was planning for their honeymoon would be fine with her. He was being very secretive about it.

Spread out before him on his desk, Scott studied the brochures of fabulous honeymoon spots. There were cruises to the Bahamas and packages for trips to Jamaica, Hawaii, Cancun, and other exotic places. None of them seemed right. Scott knew Vanessa would enjoy honeymooning at any of these beautiful vacation spots, but they were the standard, classic places people went for a honeymoon. He wanted to take her someplace different, somewhere more Nessa-like.

There was a knock at his door, and T.J. stuck his head in. "Want to join me for lunch?"

Scott cringed inside. He'd put up with T.J.'s company twice this week already—both of them were business lunches. After his remarks on Valentine's Day, Scott's attitude toward him had been cold, but professional. In a way Scott felt sorry for him. Nobody in the company seemed to be able to tolerate T.J. and avoided working with him. The other co-workers were smart. They used any excuse to steer clear of T.J.; some were pretty lame, but they worked.

It was T.J.'s own fault. He had made himself unlikable. He was always spouting one ridiculous thing or another. Since his protest about celebrating Dr. King's birthday as a holiday, he seemed more pitiful than ever.

Scott had taken offense at his remarks but thought that maybe he was more sensitive because of his relationship with

Nessa. When everyone else had tuned T.J. out, Scott had listened. Not just out of pity, but because Scott was interested in knowing his reason for protesting. He wanted to find out why an educated man in this day and age would spout such nonsense.

T.J. had explained, "I don't know why this whole office is in an uproar against me. I just thought that if this King man had a holiday, why not President Lincoln? He freed the slaves!"

Scott noticed that he'd left out the title doctor when referring to the famous civil rights leader. It was an earned title given to a very intelligent man. He realized that T.J. had done it purposely, trying to lower his importance.

Still trying to be fair, Scott listened and thought that maybe T.J. had a point—a very small point. Both men were assassinated, but Dr. King faced hatred, jail, and bombs as he fought for equal rights that should have been freely given.

Scott had no patience left and could not stomach another lunch with T.J. "No thanks, T.J. I've got an appointment to keep." He pointed to the brochures covering his desk. "Honeymoon plans."

T.J. picked up the Easter pictures of Vicki, Megan, Nessa, and Scott with the Easter Bunny. "So you're going through with it? You're really going to marry her. I thought you were only trying to…"

T.J. got no further with his comment because he happened to look up at Scott at that moment. The smile on T.J.'s face fell. "Hey, no offense, Scott. I've tried a little dark meat myself."

"You have? I find that hard to believe," Scott growled, waiting for him to go on, to say something more that would give him a good reason to smash his face in.

"I do, too. But like I said, I didn't mean any harm," he told Scott congenially. "And I had no idea how serious you were."

"Yes I am, and I suggest you remember that," Scott warned, any sympathy he had for T.J. erased by his attitude and his comments.

"She's a lovely woman," T.J sneered. "Good luck." He leaned over Scott's desk to get a look at the brochures. "Jamaica, Hawaii, Cancun, you sure you're not wasting your money?"

Scott, uncomfortable with the way T.J. had been holding onto the Easter picture, pried it out of his hand. "Keep your opinions to yourself, T.J. Like I said, I'm busy."

Still wearing a smirk, T.J. walked out. Scott thought he heard him muttering something like, "Poor man, I gotta help him out of this."

Not really surprised with his attitude and knowing that T.J. had gotten the message he silently conveyed, Scott put the incident behind him. He'd already decided to steer clear of T.J. as much as possible. His remarks assured Scott that he'd made a wise decision.

There was something very strange about him. He put the Easter picture on his desk and noticed fingerprints all over Nessa. He took a handkerchief and wiped it clean. Yes, there was definitely something wrong with T.J.

Studying the brochures again, Scott suddenly had a wonderful idea. He tossed Jamaica, Hawaii, Cancun, and all the rest into the trash can, then left for the travel agency with the perfect idea in mind.

Leaving the travel agency a half hour later with all his plans settled, Scott was in a wonderful mood for the rest of the day. In a little less than two months he'd have Nessa to himself for two whole weeks, two long pleasure-filled weeks. With thoughts of their honeymoon in mind, he couldn't wait to see her. They didn't have plans to go out tonight, but he thought he'd surprise Nessa and take her out to dinner.

As Scott pulled into his driveway that evening, he spotted a taxi driver unloading luggage onto the sidewalk. Having no idea who it could be, he was shocked to see Kathy's mother walking towards him.

"Eve, what a surprise!"

"Scott, it's so good to see you," she said, gripping his arm and dragging him forward for a choke-hug. She was a great deal smaller than Scott, but had quite a bit of strength for such a small package. Still gripping his arm, she dragged Scott to the front door talking nonstop. "I know I came unexpectedly, but when you told me you were getting married I was happy for you. I know Kathy would want you and the girls to go on with your lives. I had to meet her myself, you know. I mean, you and the girls have told me so many wonderful things about her on the phone. It was MaNessa this and MaNessa that. What an odd name, is she from here? But there's nothing like a one-on-one meeting. So I told myself..."

She continued to talk, and Scott nodded in all the right places. He knew there was no use trying to get a word in. He led Eve into the house and offered her a seat. Vicki and

Megan came running in to greet their father and were amazed to find their granny there too.

It was in the midst of the girls' excitement and Eve's rambling that Nessa walked into the house. Megan spotted her first, jumped into her arms, and yelled, "MaNessa, MaNessa, MaNessa! Look! Granny!" She pointed in the general direction of a small medium built blond-haired woman, who didn't look like anyone's granny.

Vicki ran to Vanessa, grabbed her arm, and insisted, "Come see Granny, MaNessa."

Scott had been watching the whole exchange with pride, just as anxious as the girls for Vanessa to meet Eve, so he missed the look of shock on Eve's face. He turned to Vanessa and announced, "Nessa, this is Eve Collins, Kathy's mother, and Vicki and Megan's granny."

Vanessa extended her hand in greeting. She paused when Eve exclaimed, "She's black, I mean African-American, or whatever the right word is now!"

Vanessa dropped her hand. "Yes, I am, Mrs. Collins, and you're white. And we both have two eyes, a nose, a mouth, and a brain to think with. Excuse me, please."

As she went on to the bathroom, Vanessa could hear her saying, "Oh, I'm so sorry. I didn't mean anything. I was just so surprised. Why didn't you tell me, Scott?"

"I simply didn't think to, I guess, because it doesn't matter," Vanessa heard Scott explain. "I'll be right back," was the last thing she heard Scott say. Their voices were drowned out when she turned on the faucet.

A few seconds later there was a knock on the bathroom door. "It's me, Nessa, open up."

"Me who?" she asked.

"Me, your gorgeous fiancé," he answered.

Vanessa laughed. "Well, gorgeous fiancé, I'll be out in a minute."

"You okay in there?"

"I'm fine," she assured him. "Go take care of your company."

"If you say so, but we'll be waiting for you."

She heard Scott walk away slowly, as if he still hoped she'd come out, but she made no move to follow him. Normally a harmless comment like Eve's wouldn't have bothered her. Vanessa had heard enough to be able to deal with them by now. And she knew Mrs. Collins didn't mean any harm. She simply looked surprised and probably blurted out the first thing on her mind. What had Vanessa upset was an encounter she'd had with one of her favorite cousins, Daniel.

She'd stopped to see her mom to confirm some wedding plans and was surprised when she found Danny visiting. He was a pilot and rarely in town. After handling matters with her mother, Vanessa and Danny walked to the park they'd played in as children. They both sat on a swing and talked about their jobs and general things.

Vanessa couldn't wait to tell him all about Scott and the fact that she was actually getting married. Danny used to tease her, telling her that she was too picky. He had even suggested that they get married when they were old and gray, just to keep each other company. They'd both had unsatisfactory relationships and laughed about their hopeless love lives. He was just as picky as she was.

"Danny!" she interrupted his barrage of teasing. "Haven't you heard? I'm getting married. His name's Scott, and…"

Before she could go on, Daniel finished, "And he's white."

"Yes, and he's wonderful! Danny, can you believe it? There must be some hope for you too since I've finally fallen…"

"Vanessa," he cut her off again. "Look, I came to see you, I had to know if it was true. I can't believe you're going to marry a white man."

Vanessa stared at him in confusion. "Danny, hello, where are you?" she asked, waving a hand in front of his face. "Is this my cousin, Daniel Lewis? I'm marrying a man. He happens to be the man I love! Look at me," she said getting out of the swing. "It's me, Vanessa, and I am actually in love!"

"You should be in love with a black man, okay!" he exploded as he jumped out of the swing. He stopped and stood stock-still.

Vanessa knew he was trying to calm himself down. He had a quick temper and when he got mad, he needed time to control himself. A few seconds, sometimes a few minutes, was all he needed to calm down. Vanessa waited.

He started again, slowly, calmly. "It's okay to go to school with them, to play with them, maybe even go on a date with one of them. But never, never marry one of them, Ness."

"I'm marrying a man," she let him know. "You know, the ones that have the same kind of body parts as you do."

"He's not like me," Danny insisted, his eyes full of anger.

"No, he's not," she answered calmly, worried about his reaction. Something was wrong. "I was only speaking in terms of the general male population."

"Well that's not good enough. You have to be careful, more selective."

Vanessa already knew where he was headed. She knew from the first few words that had come out of his mouth. But she wanted him to say it all. To get it out in the open. Because the words coming out of his mouth didn't sound like the Danny she knew.

"Be more selective?" she asked. "How do you know I haven't been selective? Let's see. I am marrying someone who won't beat me, he isn't a bum without a job, and he treats me like a queen. And most importantly, he loves me, and I love him right back. I didn't plan it, but that's the way love is."

"Listen Ness, I'm only trying to help you. You're marrying a man from the wrong race. You can't marry a white man."

Remembering that night on the Moonwalk, and the near attack by the two linebackers, Vanessa asked, feigning confusion, "The human race?"

The two guys on the Moonwalk were drunk. Ness wondered what was Danny's excuse. He looked frustrated, and scared, and sad all at once.

"Look, can't you just forget about this one and at least try to love a black man?" he asked her.

Vanessa stared at him. She had expected this from outsiders, but not from one of her own family. She shook her head as if to clear it. Since he let go with what was on his mind, Vanessa said what was on hers. "Danny, you act as if he's some being from another planet. You haven't listened to anything I say about him. You can't seem to get past him being white."

She waited for some kind of confirmation. When his only response was a grunt Vanessa went on. "I don't understand. Is this really you talking? Something's happened to make you think like this? Tell me about it..." she pleaded, wanting to know the real reason behind this attack.

"I just don't want you to get hurt, okay? There are guys out there, no, people out there," he corrected himself as if it made a difference. "There are people in the world that just want to experiment, try something or someone new. This one says he'll marry you, and he probably will. But he'll get tired of you and drop you like a hot potato when he's through with the experience. All I can tell you is watch out! And don't say I didn't warn you. I love you, cuz. Oh what's the use!" Daniel walked away, back towards her parents' house.

She had sat back down on the swing knowing she should let him cool off before talking to him again. She would straighten him out later. He didn't even know Scott.

Splashing water on her face, Vanessa stood and reached for a towel. She had come over to Scott's house because she didn't want to talk to her mom or Monica. What she needed was a nice bit of Scott therapy.

There was another tap on the bathroom door. She opened it to find Vicki and Megan standing on the other side with very long faces.

"Are you sad, MaNessa?" Vicki asked.

"No," she smiled. "But you two sure look down in the dumps."

Their expressions changed miraculously.

"You're not sad, good!" Vicki shouted almost hopping out of her shoes. "Come see Granny again. She wants to 'pologize."

Being led into the room by Vicki and Megan, Vanessa felt better. When Eve saw them enter the room she approached Vanessa and extended her hand in kindness.

"I think I goofed. I'm sorry. I have a big mouth and don't know how or when to use it sometimes."

"Your reaction was normal."

"But not tactful. I hope I didn't upset you."

"No, I had something else on my mind." Looking at Scott, Vanessa smiled to reassure him at his inquiring glance.

"Everything fine?" he asked.

"Yes, of course," she answered honestly since Scott was referring to the incident with Eve. "But I'm not staying." She turned to Eve. "It was nice to meet you. I hope to see you at the wedding."

"Yes, I'll be there. But don't say goodbye dear. I don't want to stop you from visiting. Please stay."

"No, I'll be on my way. I'm sure you have a lot of catching up to do, being an out-of-town grandma and all. I'll see you some time later. Scott, would you walk me to my car?" she asked, wanting just a little of that Scott therapy she was counting on.

"Wait! Wait, wait MaNessa!" Megan yelled, swinging her necklace in her chubby hand. "Sing My Sunshine, sunshine, sunshine!"

Vanessa stooped down and sang to both girls.

Eve whispered to Scott, "You always had good taste. I knew that when you married Kathy. I'm glad to see your taste hasn't changed."

Scott answered smugly, "I know a wonderful woman when I find her."

He walked Vanessa to her car then got in next to her. "Are you really okay?" he asked between the nibbles he was taking of her bottom lip.

"I'm fine. I was a little upset about something that happened earlier."

"Wanna talk about it?"

"Later, you have company. I'm sure Eve wants to spend some time with you and the girls now that she's finished checking me out."

"I was hoping to spend some time with you tonight," he told her, tracing her eyebrows and marking a trail to her ear. "But I could tell you really don't feel much like sticking around with Eve here."

"It has nothing to do with Eve, I just wanted you all to myself."

"Sorry about that, Nessa. I had the same thing in mind. Eve's coming was definitely a surprise. I'm glad you met her, but I'm sorry about the way it happened. She has a tendency to say what's on her mind, sometimes before she thinks. But she's a good person," he assured her, unable to resist tracing her left ear. "And you're right. It wasn't hard to figure the reason for her surprise visit."

"Yes, and I probably would have done the same thing if my grandchildren's father, a widower, was getting involved with someone else. I think she was probably worried about you and the girls."

"I can guarantee that she was, but Nessa, widower, you make me sound so o-l-d," Scott croaked, sounding exactly like a ninety-year-old man. "And you've made quite an impression. She's staying only until the weekend. If Eve wasn't satisfied, and I can't think of a reason she wouldn't be, she would have made plans to stay a whole lot longer. Did you see all the suitcases in the hall?"

"I noticed. It looked as if she was planning on staying for the wedding and joining us for the honeymoon, too."

They both laughed at the thought.

"I hope not," Vanessa said, a twinge of laughter still in her voice.

"There's no hope about it. It is forbidden!" he told her. "Not allowed! Taboo!"

"Just make sure she knows that."

"There's nothing to worry about my Nessa. Eve's already congratulated me on my good judgment and wishes us good luck. That also means good-bye and bon voyage."

"Does that mean we're going on a cruise for our honeymoon?"

"No, but you'll find out soon enough."

"Just make sure you're there, Scott. I might be tempted to hand out notes and pleasures to someone else."

"Don't even think that," he told her, giving her one last kiss.

Not really wanting him to leave yet, Vanessa absently played with a lock of his curly blond hair. She would like nothing better than to keep him outside just to unburden her thoughts. But just sitting and talking to him had made her feel better.

"Go on, my gorgeous fiancé. I can't keep you to myself tonight," she told him, letting Scott get back to his company. "I love you. Call me, okay?"

"I will, and don't forget we have an important errand tomorrow. We must check out our new van this weekend." Then he added with a leer and a lift of his eyebrows, "If the honeymoon's going to go as well as I plan we'll be needing that van about nine mouths later."

Late that night, Scott did call and they talked for a while, but not about what was uppermost in her mind. It wasn't something she wanted to discuss over the phone.

They made plans to spend the weekend together as usual and Vanessa had just a few days to wait. Eve would be heading home by then.

The rest of the week dragged on, and it seemed to take forever before Friday morning came. Vanessa packed a picnic lunch to surprise Scott at work since there was a half day at school. A picnic on the bayou sounded perfect. They could relax and talk without interruption.

She'd been to Scott's office a few times before, and everyone was always friendly. Not seeing his secretary, Vanessa went straight to his office and was about to knock when she was stopped by a voice.

"Scott's not in. Vanessa, isn't it?" The voice snidely asked. "Shouldn't you be somewhere teaching or something?"

Vanessa, feeling as if she was doing something illegal, turned to find T.J. standing behind her with that weird smile that always gave her the creeps. He was the one and only person in Scott's office she could not stomach. But since his father owned the company, Vanessa had decided to be cordial, if distant.

"No, I've got a half day. I wanted to surprise Scott with a picnic lunch." Not knowing why she explained all this to him, Vanessa pointed to the basket at her feet as proof.

"Oh, how nice," he said with a distinct sneer in his voice. "But I'm afraid you've just missed him. He had a business luncheon today."

Disappointed, Vanessa turned to leave. "Just tell him I came by then. I'll be on my way."

"Let me help you with the basket."

Not wanting him to get too close, Vanessa reached for the basket only to have him take it from her.

"I'll walk you to your car," he offered, guiding her in the direction of the door. He suddenly seemed anxious to get rid of her.

Not as anxious as she was to get away from him. She groaned inside when he continued talking in a conversational tone.

"Congratulations on your up and coming marriage. But I am so sorry to see that you can't possibly have any serious feelings for Scott. Otherwise you'd do what's best for him and…" he stopped, letting the rest hang in the air. "I'm sorry, I shouldn't have said that. Perhaps I'm being too forward."

He really didn't sound sorry, and Vanessa didn't want to ask what he meant. She knew she'd be sorry if she did. People weren't as closed-minded as he implied. But out of curiosity the question just slipped out, "And exactly what do you mean by that?"

"I didn't want to say this. I don't like to butt in other people's business, but remember you asked," he told her, trying to appear reluctant. "It's just, the way I see it, if you're going to marry him you can't possibly be in love with him," T.J. answered as if it made perfect sense.

Realizing what he was referring to but pretending not to follow his line of thought Vanessa said, "Last time I heard, marriage and love went hand in hand."

"Normally, I'd say, yes it does, but not when it interferes with a man's career and dreams. I mean, the whole race issue could cause anything to happen. In this line of work, there's a great deal of socializing, and some people tend to get offended if they see an unnatural couple. I mean, Scott can't possibly socialize in the same circles with a black wife!"

Unnatural? The only thing unnatural right now was the intrusion T.J was making into their private life. What right did he have? Who did he think he was? Why was she even standing here listening to him? Vanessa was beginning to get angry, the surprise at his audacity having worn off. Grabbing the picnic basket out of his hand she turned to put it back into the car. Suddenly remembering that T.J. was the boss's son, she turned back and demanded, "When you say anything, I think you need to be more specific."

Leaning on her car, T.J. crossed his arms and nonchalantly informed her, "I can be more specific. Let's see, he might not move up the ladder of success and who knows, he could even lose his job. It would be such a waste. Scott's a very talented architect. Oh well, you never know…"

Fully understanding now the reason why she was always uncomfortable around this jerk, Vanessa left in a hurry. She knew she could scream lawsuit if he acted on any of his subtle threats. But was it worth it? This whole situation could open a can of worms and turn Scott's life, and the girls', upside down and inside out.

Just coming from a meeting with Travis Sr., Scott found it odd to see T.J. coming into the office building. He'd excused himself from the meeting ten minutes earlier and hadn't returned.

"Had some kind of emergency?" Scott asked.

"Oh, yeah, but everything's taken care of, and you're gonna thank me for it later, buddy."

Scott didn't understand a word and saw no need to decipher T.J.'s ramblings since he was determined to keep his distance. Scott turned to his secretary and asked for messages, hoping to have gotten one from Nessa.

"No messages since I left to find those figures for you, and nothing on the machine," she answered.

"Okay, thanks," Scott said, disappointed. But with this being Friday, he knew he'd see her later. And if he worked through his lunch hour, he could knock off early and maybe spend an hour or so alone with her before he went home to relieve the babysitter. Smiling at the thought, Scott got busy.

CHAPTER TWENTY-THREE

Writing that letter was the hardest thing she had ever done in her life. But Vanessa knew it was necessary. She wrote it because she loved Scott and refused to be a hindrance in his life. Since it seemed that she couldn't become a part of his life without causing problems and upheavals, Vanessa was prepared to give him up.

She didn't make this decision solely based on T.J. and his nasty remarks, although those did weigh heavily on her mind. In the past few days the fears and anxieties, which she had believed she'd overcome, came crashing back. Talking with Daniel, meeting Eve Collins, and the confrontation with T.J. resurrected the fears she had kept hidden deep down inside her—the uncertainty, the knowledge that she might not be able to handle it.

She didn't want to put Scott through any unnecessary problems, so there was nothing she could do but tell him good-bye. She couldn't deal with it, so it was her problem.

Vanessa's body shuddered with a sigh of sadness. She couldn't face him because he'd only make her give in. It was better this way. It was also cowardly, she knew, but her plan was to sneak the letter into his mailbox.

She took her bike down to ride over to Scott's house. She didn't want the girls to hear her car and come out. The girls...Vicki and Megan...how she wanted to be their mother. They'd be heartbroken. But Vanessa didn't let herself think about her desertion. If she thought too much about leaving them, she wouldn't go through it. And this situation would only be more heartbreaking in the long run for all of them. Breaking the engagement and leaving Scott was best for everyone.

She had to leave the letter before Scott got home from work.

Not remembering exactly how she made her way there, Vanessa found herself in Scott's driveway. She got off the bike on stiff legs, walked to the mailbox, lifted the lid, and added her letter to the mail already inside.

She quickly walked back to her bike, hopped on, and rode to the end of the driveway only to be stopped by the sight of Scott driving down the street.

Not waiting for Vanessa to move out of the driveway he pulled up, blocking her escape route.

"What a nice surprise!" he said jumping out of the car. "You have no idea how much I've missed you."

He guided her bike up the driveway and into the garage. Vanessa couldn't protest. This would be their last time together, their last moment of pleasure, her chance to say good-bye. Two seconds later, Vanessa had backed Scott against the wall and used her entire body to show him how much she loved him. Her lips, hands and hips all moved in a rhythm that seemed to shout: I love you. I can't tell you enough, how much I love you.

"My God, Nessa!" Scott breathed in heavily, holding her tightly against his chest. "I missed you too, but we've got less than two months of waiting. I figure that's about forty-five days, a little over six weeks, close to one thousand-eight hours. Should I go into minutes and seconds, teach? I've been counting those too." He caressed her shoulders, realizing how tense she was.

Full of built up tension himself, Scott told her, "If you keep this up, I won't be able to wait another second." Leaning back a little he brushed the hair out of her eyes and smiled when he realized that he really wanted to wait despite the constant temptation. "Our wedding night is going to be so special."

Suddenly Vanessa wished she'd never made Scott promise to wait. Then she'd at least have made love to him. Maybe now, here. Desperate, Vanessa yanked at his shirt, pulling Scott toward her, causing buttons to pop off. "I don't want to wait anymore. Make love to me, Scott. Right now! Right this minute!"

Scott pulled back, determined to get a good look at her face. He was worried. Something was definitely wrong.

"Nessa, what's gotten into you? I will not make love to you in a garage. You're going to be my wife before that happens." For a man who'd been in a constant state of arousal for three months that was a huge statement. And he knew he meant it. Now was not the time. Scott wanted their vows said and a commitment made before they had their honeymoon.

"What is it?" he asked, trying to understand the desperation he saw in her face. "Is it that you can't resist your gorgeous fiancé one minute longer?" he joked, trying to coax a smile.

He didn't get a smile. Instead he got a sound out of her that was a cross between a laugh and a moan.

Feeling that she needed some Scott therapy, he gathered her into his arms again.

Scott moved in a rocking motion, comforting her like he would his daughters. He didn't know what was wrong, but it felt good to hold her in his arms. He began to hum a tune.

Oh, this is so sweet, Vanessa thought. This is what I'm leaving behind. She would enjoy this moment now, and cry later.

Not knowing how long he held her, but feeling a subtle change, Scott tilted her head up and asked, "Better?"

"I guess so. I don't think that things could get any worse." Oh, how true that was she thought.

"I hope not," he told her, peering into her face again. "Do you know what it does to me to know that you want me as much as I want you? And I'm not just talking about my male ego here. My heart swells with love for you, my Nessa. It's our time remember?" He took off the watch he always wore, turning it over to show her the inscription they both knew by heart: our love was a near collision.

"Like you said, there was a time for us to meet and fall in love." When she only looked up at him, he continued, "We made a promise together, and we're going to keep on waiting for the right time to make love. And every second that we wait builds up such sweet anticipation that neither one of us will regret it."

Regrets, there were so many regrets she was going to have, but Vanessa was still determined to do what she felt she needed to do. Not being able to look at him without those regrets plastered all over her face, Vanessa stepped out of his embrace and turned away from him. She stared at the cement floor of the garage.

Thinking she was disappointed, Scott reached over and wrapped his arms around her. He tried to cheer her up. "My Nessa, don't forget that there's still a wide variety of pleasures we haven't experienced yet."

"I know, it's just that I really do want you, Scott." She soaked up his embrace and without turning around voiced her deepest feelings. "I love you, Scott."

"And I love you, my Nessa."

She turned to take in her fill. "But I'd better head on home before I lose control again." And cry all over you, she silently added.

"Did you come to see the girls?" he asked. "I got off early and was only driving by before coming out to your house when I spotted you. How about spending some time with your gorgeous fiancé first?"

Drinking in the sight of him again, Vanessa thought, he is gorgeous with those smoky gray eyes, curly hair, and that adorable dimple. And he was mine, but not anymore.

She heard herself answer, "I need to shower first, and I want to take my bike home."

"Then you don't want a lift? I could put the bike in the trunk."

"No." She forced herself to resist the temptation to spend just a little more time with him. "I think I need the physical exercise. It'll help burn off this extra energy." She was turning out to be a pretty good liar because she felt more drained than anything right now which was why she couldn't look him in the face.

"Are you sure?"

"Yes," she looked down, uncomfortable with her lie.

Scott didn't look convinced, but held the bike for her. "We'll talk later then. And don't forget we're going to the car dealership tomorrow. We want to have enough room for all those children we'll have."

"I won't forget." Vanessa got onto her bike and waved good-bye. She felt the heartbreak all the way down to her toes. She could barely pedal knowing that there wouldn't be any children with Scott, ever.

Controlling her sorrow by simply not thinking at all, Vanessa rode on. Her feet guided her to the lake. She found her place on the levee. The same place where she wished upon a star. The place where she thought her wish had come true. But reality invaded and mined her dreams.

Vanessa sat, put her head on her knees, and released the flood of emotion she held back during her ride here. She sat crying and staring at the horizon for hours. It was long after sundown when she finally moved from her perch on the levee. She couldn't go home. She knew Scott would be there waiting.

After Vanessa rode away Scott didn't let her strange mood bother him. Whatever it was that was bothering her, she'd eventually tell him. He was hoping it was nothing more serious than wedding jitters.

Before he could get to the front door it opened. Megan, Vicki, and Miss Laura, the sitter, came out. They were so concerned about getting the mail that they didn't notice him standing at the edge of the driveway.

"My turn, my turn, my turn!" Megan yelled.

"What should you say?" Miss Laura asked.

"Please, please, please!" Megan answered.

"Okay," Miss Laura agreed. "I'll hold you up, but you have to pass them to Vicki."

They'd just finished getting all the mail out when Vicki noticed Scott.

"Daddy!" she shouted, running up to him.

"Down, Miz Laura!" Megan pleaded. "Daddy, Daddy, Daddy!"

The girls were picked up by their dad, who pretended to be a weightlifter.

"See, Miss Laura, I'm Mr. Muscle Dad!"

The girls giggled as Scott moved them up and down.

"Just make sure you don't drop the weights, Mr. Muscle Dad," Miss Laura commented in her frank way.

"Of course not. Not my lovely ladies." Scott set them down and they ran inside. "Since I'm home early, you can leave as soon as you're ready."

Reaching inside the front door to grab her purse, Laura answered, "Then I'm leaving. I'll see you Monday, Muscles. Bye-bye girls!" she called while walking out the door.

Good-byes could be heard coming from inside. The sitter had been working out really well. But they wouldn't need her for most of the summer. After their honeymoon, Vanessa planned to be home with the girls all summer long, and then they'd be starting pre-school at St. Ann's. Of course, Laura still offered to be available to them whenever they needed her.

When Scott walked inside, Vicki was on the living room floor sorting the mail according to size, small envelopes to magazines.

"Look Daddy, this one doesn't have a picture."

"You mean it doesn't have a stamp," he answered as he looked at the envelope.

"Yeah, but there's a letter S on it. It's for you, Daddy!"

Vicki thought anything with an S belonged to him. It didn't matter if it was mail or a Snicker's bar. If it started with an S, it was for him. And this one really was, because his name was written on the envelope. He recognized Nessa's neat script—that perfect teacher's handwriting. Knowing that she'd probably just put it in the mailbox, Scott believed it some kind of love note, another pleasure.

He sat the girls in front of the television to watch their favorite video, Winnie the Pooh. Filled with anticipation, he went into his room. This would be his first love note from Nessa. When he sat on his bed to read it, Scott was stunned.

Dear Scott,

I love you.

But I can't marry you. Goodbye forever,

Vanessa

He stared at the short note in disbelief. How could she dismiss him—them—with a three-lined note? There was no explanation, nothing—just three lines full of contradictions.

He sat for a long time reading the note again and again. Disbelief turned into anger. If Nessa thought that was the end of it, she'd better think again. Scott was determined to get to the bottom of this. This explained her funny mood. It wasn't wedding jitters. It was wedding dumping! What about their love for each other?

First, he called Wendy to ask her to keep the girls for the night. He didn't go into any details, just told her something important had come up.

Winnie the Pooh was ending when Scott came into the den to get the girls.

"Daddy, Daddy, Daddy, I want MaNessa," Megan demanded.

"Me too," Vicki added.

"I know." I want to see Nessa too, he silently added. "But right now you two are going to see Aunt Wendy." Trying to sound enthusiastic Scott added, "And you get to spend the night." They usually loved to spend the night at Wendy's, so Scott was hoping to distract them with that treat.

Vicki, more cautious in accepting this change in their usual routine asked, "Can I still see MaNessa later?"

"We'll see, Vicki. Sometime soon."

Vicki seemed to be satisfied with that answer. "Okay, Daddy, we can do now," she graciously allowed.

After leaving the girls at Wendy's, Scott felt calm enough to speak to Vanessa rationally. But when he got to her house, Vanessa wasn't there—only her car, he discovered, after knocking on the door and peering through every window.

Realizing that she was still on her bike, Scott sat in one of the lawn chairs and waited. For an hour he sat there waiting, playing and replaying scenes in his mind of how best to approach Nessa. Should he be angry and demanding, or patient and understanding? Remembering her strange behavior, he decided patience was his best route.

For the next hour he paced up and down her block, waiting, practicing the virtue of patience, and thinking of words of understanding. Words like...I know you must be upset. Or, how can I help? We can work it out...

He stopped pacing when he saw a curtain flutter in the window across the street. He knew the neighbors must think he was a madman pacing up and down the sidewalk. They'd probably call the police soon. Besides that, the patience he was practicing was wearing thin and frustration was taking its place. If only he knew what she was thinking.

Deciding not to give up, Scott went to the back of her apartment. He remembered a window with a broken latch that he had warned her to get fixed. Scott hoped the landlord hadn't gotten around to repairing it yet. Relieved that her landlord's house seemed deserted, he looked around cautiously, then lifted the window. Being careful, Scott moved the plants Nessa purposely left on the window ledge. He crawled through noiselessly—but unfortunately not unseen.

"Hey, Mr. Scott, what's up?" Sabrina asked, peering into the window. "Miss Vanessa lost her keys or something?"

"Something like that," Scott answered, rising from his crouched position on the floor. Did the kid ever stay in her house?

"I just came over to see if you guys would like to buy some tickets to our band's spring concert? I'm in the concert band. Did Miss Vanessa ever tell you that?"

"I don't think so. But I'll ask her, and we'll get back to you later, okay?"

"Okay, thanks," Sabrina replied looking around, obviously not ready to leave yet. "Is there anything I can do to help?"

"No. No, thank you. I've got it covered." *Go home,* he added silently. *Just go home, kid.*

"Mr. Scott?"

"Yes, Sabrina," he answered, hoping this would be her final question. This was getting to him.

"Josh and John aren't with you, are they?"

"No."

"Of course not, why would I be so lucky," she muttered, finally turning away and starting toward her own yard. "Miss Vanessa's got a boyfriend hanging around, kissing her like crazy, and sneaking into her house…"

Scott shut the window, then walked through each of Nessa's rooms. He found no sign of her, just as he had suspected. Her bike was gone, which confirmed that she was still out riding. Where could she be? The sun had gone down half an hour ago.

Thinking that she might have gone to her parents' or Monica's, Scott called and asked if they'd seen Nessa. Both assumed she was with him, so Nessa must have kept this breakup to herself. Scott hoped she continued to do just that. Because whether she realized it or not, she would become Mrs. Scott Halloway. There was going to be a June wedding and a honeymoon, just like they planned. Knowing he wouldn't see her this night Scott left a note. One he was sure Nessa would understand.

> *Dear Nessa,*
>
> > *Our time is now. I love you.*
> > *I know you'll keep your promise to marry me.*
> > *Yours forever and ever,*
>
> *Scott*

Feeling a little better but still anxious about Nessa being out at night on her bike, Scott left the house putting the plants back where they belonged. He went out the front door and made sure it locked behind him. He went to his car and parked a discreet distance away on a curve hidden behind some bushes. Vanessa would have to look hard to find him. After waiting another half an hour, he was relieved to see her slowly pedaling toward her apartment. She was looking around, obviously searching for signs of him. He waited a few minutes then drove past, noticing her lights on. By now, she must have seen his note. He'd left it hanging by a long strip of tape in her bedroom doorway. She couldn't miss it.

He drove home knowing deep inside that everything was going to be okay. Stopping at a red light behind a sports car, Scott read the personalized license plate. It said JESS4ME. And he thought, that's right, she's "just for me." From the top of her head, with the short black hair that framed her beautiful face with those expressive brown eyes, down to those long, sexy legs that drove him crazy. It was simple, she was just right for him, and he was just right for her. Surely she could not have forgotten that.

Remembering that the car salesman had offered to personalize the license plate on their new van, Scott had a brilliant idea.

CHAPTER TWENTY-FOUR

Avoiding Scott became very difficult, not because she had a problem dodging him physically, but purely emotionally. At home she had removed all traces of Scott and anything that would remind her of him. She put her bicycle in her landlord's garage so she wouldn't have to look at it every time she walked out the door. She even took her Cupids off the night stand next to her bed. She'd put them in the top drawer of her dresser, face down and covered by some clothes. If she didn't see them every morning and every night she'd be able to handle this better. Vanessa knew a cut and dried break-off was best, but Scott was making it difficult.

First there was the note. Vanessa cried all night after reading that note. She knew Scott deserved some explanation, and that she had hurt him. She just couldn't give him one, and it made the situation worse that he wasn't giving up. Every morning for the past week there had been a note written on heart-shaped paper, telling Vanessa how much he loved her. He never demanded to see her or came knocking at her door. He just left those heartbreaking love notes. She had to admit, it was getting harder and harder to resist contacting him and throwing all her anxieties right out the window. But she couldn't.

And then there were the lunches. Vanessa drove to work that morning wondering what Scott would bring to her today. All morning during reading, spelling, and language lessons, she wondered—especially when she took her students to lunch.

She went down the hall to the teachers' lounge still thinking about Scott, hoping she wouldn't run into him in the hall. He'd personally brought her lunch to work every day via the school office. It had nothing to do with feeding her stomach to get to her heart. Rather it showed just how sweet and wonderful he was. Scott knew it was next to impossible to get to use the one and only microwave oven in the teacher's lounge and still have time to eat in a thirty-minute lunch period.

It was such a thoughtful gift. On Monday, he brought finger sandwiches, Tuesday Chinese, Wednesday a shrimp po-boy dressed with lots of lettuce and tomatoes, just the way she liked it. And on Thursday he brought a steaming hot Mexican plate. Written somewhere on each package were the words YOURS FOREVER, SCOTT.

Vanessa was touched, but she barely ate any of the delicious food. Instead, she sat in a corner of the teachers' lounge and usually ended up giving away most of the meal. But she always kept the bag or container with Scott's name on it.

By Friday everyone in the school, teachers and office staff alike, were wondering what Scott would bring. Vanessa listened to the speculation as she bought a drink out of the machine in the lounge. Of course no one knew she'd broken off her engagement with Scott. They just assumed he was being sweet.

"What do you think he'll bring today, Vanessa?" one coworker asked.

"I bet he's going to wrap himself in a big plastic bag and wait for you by your classroom door, then you can have him for lunch," another teacher suggested, making everyone laugh.

"I bet she won't share, then." teased the assistant principal.

Not putting a gag like that past Scott, Vanessa quickly left the lounge. Turning toward the school office, she spotted the back of Scott's head. He was just leaving. Vanessa stood and watched as he walked down the hallway. Her heart ached at the sight of him. She wanted to race after him, throw her arms around him...

She went into the office and picked up the lunch Scott had delivered. "That's one fine young man you have there," the secretary said.

Vanessa went into her classroom instead of the lounge. She wasn't in the mood for more of the good-natured teasing she knew would continue if she went back into the room full of teachers. Vanessa sat at her desk and opened the Styrofoam container. It was a seafood dinner. Shrimp, oysters, fish, fries, and toast, all warm and golden brown. It smelled so good. But Vanessa didn't feel like eating. She found his signature, tore it off and put it in her purse with the others. Vanessa shuddered and wondered how she was going to get through this.

Scott went past the teachers' lounge as he had done all week, but Vanessa was nowhere around. He felt ridiculous peering through the window and not finding her there. Where else could she have gone? Her classroom, he thought and moved quickly to the other side of the building. Scott looked into her classroom, thankful that it was on the first floor. He watched her for a minute as he'd done each day. He saw her put a piece of paper into her purse. He smiled smugly and turned to leave. He knew it wouldn't be long now. She was still upset and confused, he just had to find out why. That was next to impossible since she hadn't confided in her family. He called a few times at her parents' and Monica's to find out if Nessa had said anything to them. But they only commented on missing them last Sunday and were expecting a visit next week.

On one of those calls to Nessa's parents, Josh had answered the phone. "How about a little one on one, brother-in-law?" he had asked. "Or are those old bones too tired and brittle to take me on?"

It had been on the tip of Scott's tongue to laugh him off and refuse. But thinking Josh and his twin brother might be a good source of information, Scott agreed. Not to play one on one, but some two on two. Josh and John against him and Jack. Scott figured he and Jack would teach those two youngsters a little lesson while he pumped them for information.

Since Jack had a membership, they met at the Lee Circle Y on the edge of the Central Business District. The YMCA faced a large circular park that the St. Charles streetcar line circled on its daily rounds. In the center of the park was a huge statue of Robert E. Lee, distinguishing this Y from the others in the greater New Orleans area.

Scott dropped the girls off to spend the morning with Wendy and the boys then took off with Jack. They were able to park right in front of the Lee Circle Y, where Josh and John were waiting outside dribbling the ball up and down the block, full of energy.

Jack yawned. "Tell me again why we're doing this?"

"To teach two cocky almost twenty-somethings a lesson."

"And what's that lesson?" Jack opened the van door. "That we're not that old? Not good enough, Scott. I am getting old. So old I could fall asleep right here, right now, without a second thought."

"Alright then, how about this. To make us feel as young and cocky as those two out there," Scott told him, pointing his head in the direction of the energetic twins. "We have to stay in shape, Jack. When was the last time we played? A month ago?"

Jack yawned again, eyeing Josh's and John's seemingly unlimited supply of energy. "And this is how we make up for it? We dive right in to get slaughtered?"

Scott got out of the van. "It won't be so bad. Let's go show them what a couple of thirty-somethings can do!"

"Oh yeah!" Jack caught up with Scott. "We can show 'em how good we pant, fall, and bleed."

The twins met them. "All right!" said Josh. "We thought you two might have chickened out."

"No way, we had to save face." Scott decided to start the probing right away and added, "If Nessa found out I was too scared to play a little basketball, she wouldn't let me hear the end if it."

"You know Ness's not like that," John had reminded him. "If anything she'd jump on us for raggin' you into playing. You know how protective she is!"

"But that wouldn't have stopped us," said Josh. "Besides, Ness doesn't need to know a thing. With all those plans she's drowning in for the wedding, and those midterms we've finally finished, we haven't seen her in a couple of weeks."

They hadn't seen Ness in the last two weeks. With that little newsflash, the probing was complete. Scott had gotten the information he was after, and some added insight. Nessa was trying to protect him. That had to be it. But from what? He still had to figure that one out. Now that he had the information he was looking for, Scott wondered if he could get out of actually playing against these two hot shots.

"Heads up!" Josh shouted, passing the ball to Scott. "Let's play some ball."

Th e was no graceful way out. Both he and Jack had discovered that when thirty-somethings play against almost twenty-somethings the older guys panted, fell, and bled real good. They also weren't as fast across that court. With an embarrassing score of sixty-two to ten, Scott vowed not to play against the twins again—until he was in much better shape.

That had been five days ago, and Scott's muscles were still sore. Driving away from the school building and back to work in the new mini van, he felt some of his tension ease. With Nessa keeping those pieces of paper and her family not knowing what was going on, he was confident that he'd win her back, despite the fact that the only thing he could find out was that she was protecting him. He'd know it all soon enough through patience.

Whistling as he walked back into the office, Scott waved as he passed T.J.

He followed Scott inside. "Well, it's good to see you back to your old self."

Scott frowned. "My old self?"

T.J. wasn't put off by Scott's lack of attention, he couldn't wait to tell him. "And you've got me to thank for it," T.J. gloated. "After all I put the right bug in her ear, and you've bounced right back. In less than a week, I might add."

Scott stared at him uncomprehendingly. What was he talking about? Whatever it was, he seemed to be proud of it. Well, T.J. was a co-worker, if an irritating one. The least he could do was listen to the guy brag about his achievements. Scott was sure nobody else would.

Scott's mind was slow to work but snatches of what T.J. said finally cut through.

"And be smart," T.J. ended as if he was imparting a pearl wisdom. "Choose one that's the right color next time."

Scott didn't stop to think; he didn't need to. T.J. didn't have time to react, but probably wished he had. He grabbed T.J. by the shoulders and slammed him against the office door, closing it for privacy. Here was the reason for his problems. He just knew it. This was what Nessa had been protecting him from.

Patience, a voice said inside him. *Patience is a virtue. Hear him out.* But he had to admit he was not feeling very virtuous.

"What bug, and whose ear?" Scott demanded.

"Now, Scott," T.J. gulped, "calm down. I know you weren't really serious about marrying that ni…"

The pride, the cockiness, and the smirk T.J. always wore were gone from his face. He looked suddenly very nervous.

"Don't say it," Scott warned as he pushed him harder against the door. "Or you're gonna be a pitiful sight." Leaning closer and carefully enunciating each word with controlled fury, Scott demanded, "Now, when did you see Nessa, and exactly what did you say to her?"

With droplets of sweat running down his pasty-white face, T.J. recounted his meeting with Vanessa.

Scott tightened his grip on the man. "Was that everything?"

"Y-y-yeah," T.J. stammered with a look of fear in his eyes. "Let me go. You're a maniac, and I'll report you to my father."

"Go right ahead. Just so you know, I never liked you before, and I can't stand you now. Stay away from me and anyone or anything that has a remote connection to me. And if I hear another racial slur from you, you will find yourself in court. I decide who becomes a part of my life. I choose whom I want to marry, is that clear?"

T.J. nodded and, as soon as Scott loosened his grip, tore open the office door. "Just wait till you see what happens when my dad hears about this!"

That did it. Scott swung and connected with bone. There was a loud crack, then a look of extreme pain on T.J.'s face.

"Now, get out of here!"

T.J. did not have to be told twice.

Still angry, Scott didn't care what T.J. would do. He had a thing or two to say to Travis Sr. when he came back from his business trip. Travis would be lucky if Scott decided to stay after this insult. His reputation was such that he could choose to work anywhere.

Falling into his leather chair, Scott stared at the Easter picture on his desk. Some of his frustration eased. Just looking at the picture seemed to help. He could see in his mind other pictures, just like this, taken in the years to come.

Scott told his secretary to hold any calls, then leaned back, trying to think. He needed to see Nessa, talk with her. Now that he knew what was bothering her, it wouldn't take much to reassure her.

Or would it?

He'd find out. The main thing was to see her face to face. To talk some sense into her. To remind her of the strength and quality of their love for each other.

He'd call her. No. He'd see her as soon as she got home from school.

CHAPTER TWENTY-FIVE

Vannesa needed to get away, even if it was only for a few hours. Her mind was full of Scott—her head, full of questions she couldn't deal with answering. Was she making a mistake? Was she being too sensitive? Too insecure? Or just a complete coward?

A few hours spent in a dark, cool movie theater would be a good escape. As soon as the school day was over, Vanessa went straight to the movies. To kill time she decided to go to the Esplanade Mall in Kenner, a city outside New Orleans. Avoiding the interstate Vanessa drove at a moderate speed. The forty-five minute ride somehow relaxed her. Her mind focused on nothing more than stop lights, the busy street, and fellow road travelers.

She lost herself in the action of the film. Watching the main character pull himself out of one perilous predicament after another kept thoughts of her own problems far away. Since it was so effective, Vanessa sat through the movie twice, not leaving the theater until long after the sun had gone down.

She crossed the parking lot and went inside the mall. Vanessa wandered up and down passing the many businesses on both floors of the huge building, not really focusing on anything in particular. She ate a chicken breast sandwich in the food court for lack of anything else to do, and was forced to leave when the mall closed.

When she got home Vanessa unplugged the phone, showered, and immediately got into bed. The block that had given her brain a much-needed rest slowly disappeared.

Her last thoughts as she drifted off to sleep were of course...of Scott. She dreamed of him.

Morning came quickly and Vanessa couldn't remember any of the details of her dreams. The images in her mind were fuzzy and unclear, which was exactly how she felt about the decision she had made. But there was one thing she knew for sure, that Scott was in her dreams...he was there.

Last night her mind might have been clear and free from thought, but this morning thinking was all she could do. Vanessa thought of ways she could explain her actions to Scott without the risk of him changing her mind in one minute, only to be unsure for the rest her life. She thought of her family who knew nothing of her plans to cancel the wedding. She didn't know how to tell them.

All day long as she cleaned her apartment and washed clothes, she mentally made lists to help organize her thoughts. The pros and cons of giving Scott up, of telling her family, of marrying Scott, and even running away with him to live on a deserted island.

She left her house later that Saturday evening to go to vigil mass in an attempt to avoid Scott, and also any and all of her family. She felt as if she'd gone through every detail from start to finish only to begin again, moving in circles. She was getting no where. She went to bed that night with that thought and dreamed of Scott again.

Vanessa woke up late Sunday morning. Having already gone to mass and no intentions of going to her parents house she decided that hanging around her apartment wasn't helping. She got herself up and moving and went for a walk.

She strolled to City Park, ignoring the antics of the squirrels and the quacking of the ducks. Vanessa was so wrapped up in her misery that she didn't hear her name being called. It wasn't until someone nearly ran over her with a bike, that Vanessa saw her friend, Jessica.

By the time they finished hugging, Jessica's husband, Adam, and their twin daughters arrived on the scene. The girls were four years old and adorable. They reminded Vanessa of Vicki and Megan. And she didn't want to be reminded. She felt awful for leaving them and tried to push all thoughts of her desertion to the back of her mind.

The girls ran to the playground equipment while the adults sat on a nearby bench. Vanessa watched how Adam comfortably sat down next to his wife. They weren't concerned about anyone but each other and their daughters. That was just how she and Scott were not long ago, Vanessa thought. Until she realized that she wasn't strong enough to handle it.

She looked at her friend. Jessica was a short, petite ball of energy. Adam called her his little tootsie roll because her complexion was as dark as chocolate, and she was short and as sweet as candy. Adam on the other hand was tall and thin with a fair-complexion and sandy-blond hair. He was so laid back sometimes Vanessa thought he was asleep. They seemed to be complete opposites from the color of their skin to their personalities, but they certainly looked happy.

Drawing his attention away from his daughters, Adam asked, "So how are things going, Ness? I hear you're getting married."

"Tell us all about him, Ness," Jessica invited.

Vanessa, unable to control herself, burst out crying and spilled the whole story.

Adam and Jessica listened without interrupting, and when Vanessa was all talked out, Adam gave her his handkerchief. He said, "I know you feel that you've done the right thing, but if you love this man you'd better do your best to keep him, not leave him."

"We've learned, Ness, that you will encounter ignorance and bigotry, no matter where you go, no matter what you do. But you've got to live your life the way you want to. That includes loving and marrying the man you want. And we're talking from experience here," Jessica added, glancing at her husband.

"And you have to realize something, we're not the ones with the problem. We love each other." Adam squeezed his wife's hand. "It's other people who have a problem seeing us together, and they have to deal with it."

"So, Ness, go back to your man, talk to him," Jessica insisted.

Vanessa knew she was discussing her problem with the right people. Who would know better all the problems involved in an inter-racial marriage than people who lived with it daily.

"Monica told me something like this months ago. But I don't know if I can handle it. It's not so much people looking at us curiously, or even the rude comments behind our backs. I know the whole world isn't against us…it's not any of that. What I cannot handle is being the cause of any problems that would hurt Scott."

"Ness," Adam said. "I don't know Scott, but by not discussing this with him you cause him more hurt than anything you two would have to face together. What we do, and what you'll have to do, is to tackle one problem at a time."

"You're strong enough to deal with it." Jessica put an arm around Vanessa and gave her an encouraging squeeze. "The question is do you love him enough to deal with it?"

Of course she loved him enough. Jessica believed she was also strong enough. But the question was: did she?

When her friends left, Vanessa sat for a while letting their advice sink in. It made sense, but she wasn't confident that she could deal with the kind of problems the T.J.s of the world would throw in their path.

Glad that she'd gone out, and even happier that she'd run into Jessica and Adam, Vanessa actually noticed the squirrels playing, and the ducks quacking. She felt better, but she hadn't made any decisions yet.

Even though it was early, when Vanessa got home she decided to take a bubble bath and spend the evening watching TV. If she emptied her mind now she might be able to think more clearly later. As she got into the tub Vanessa couldn't help but imagine sharing it with Scott. That would have been an interesting pleasure, one she would have reserved for after they were married.

Married…so much for clearing her mind.

Vanessa soaked in the tub for over an hour. Inspecting her wrinkled fingers, she decided it was time to get out. She felt relaxed but a little lightheaded from being in the hot tub. As she walked into the kitchen there was a knock on the front door. She froze, thinking it might be Scott.

It was.

CHAPTER TWENTY-SIX

"Open up, Nessa. It's me," Scott said.

"I know."

"We need to talk. I've given you some time and space, but now we need to talk."

"I know that, too."

"Then why is the door still closed?"

"Because I'm scared."

"I can fix that. That's why I'm here."

Vanessa opened the door. "I knew you'd say that, that's one of the reasons I'm scared." Vanessa stood in the doorway staring at her gorgeous...ex-fiancé. She didn't like the sound of that word.

She stepped back. Scott walked in, shutting the door behind him. He stood where he was, leaning against the door with that intense look in his eyes. "Maybe that should be the first thing we discuss. You don't have any reason to ever be afraid of me, Nessa. I love you."

"I know."

"And you love me, too."

"Scott, I know that, too. Please stop. Give me a chance to say something more."

"Okay," he agreed, folding his arms. "That's why I'm here."

"I'm not afraid of you. I've never been afraid of you. But, I am scared of disappointing you...of hurting you."

"That doesn't make sense. I'm hurting right now." His hands dropped to his side.

He was. Vanessa could see it in his eyes. "I'm scared of hurting you more."

Reaching out to gently touch her shoulders he explained, "How can I hurt any more? The woman I love has left me, with no explanation, just a little note. And in that note what does she reveal? That she stills love me!"

"That's never been a doubt, but our racial difference can cause..."

"T.J.!"

"You know about T.J.?"

"Yes I do," he told her softly. "And I don't understand how you let that snake and his venom come between us. Why didn't you come to me?"

"Scott, I wanted to, but this is what I was afraid of."

His hands fell from her shoulders. "What? That I'd understand and want to protect you?"

"Yes, that you would be understanding and protective, and then I'd feel that everything was okay. But what happens if another T.J. comes along? Then another, and another. What next? I don't want to put you through a life of constantly wondering who's ready to attack you because of our relationship. I'm not strong enough to deal with that, Scott." She rubbed her eyes with the palm of her hand. She hadn't been ready to face him. He'd never seen her cry before.

Scott pulled her close and held her tight. "You are a strong woman, Vanessa Lewis," he whispered in her ear. "And we can do this together."

Scott therapy, she thought, and it was working. She could feel herself melt against him and the turmoil inside her dissolving. It was working too well. Vanessa pulled away from him. "I need more time, Scott. I'm not as sure as you are."

"Time. Okay," he agreed, frustration in his voice. "I can give you a little more time. But there's one thing that you have to remember." His voice softened. "Nothing can come between us, My Nessa. You are my heart, my soul, and the music in my life."

With that, he kissed her softly before walking out the door.

Scott got into the van and drove home. It had taken three frustrating days to finally see her. Three days of unanswered phone calls and knocking on her apartment. And still, nothing was resolved. At least his suspicions were confirmed. She was doubting herself and protecting him. Somehow, he had to make her see that there was no need to do either.

Scott went into his house, grateful to find it quiet. He thanked Laura for coming to baby-sit on a Sunday evening. She had even bathed the girls and tucked them into bed. He went into their room. Vicki was holding the locket Nessa had given her for Valentine's Day. Megan had hers wrapped around her teddy bear's neck, nearly smothering him as she slept. The Sunshine Song and those lockets were the only things keeping them from declaring out and out war on him, demanding that they be taken to MaNessa immediately.

As a matter of fact, while he was on the phone trying yet again to reach Nessa, Vicki did create a mild upstart last night. She and Megan had packed their Winnie the Pooh backpacks and, wearing their lockets, marched up to him. Vicki, the spokeswoman, told him, "Take us to MaNessa now or Megan'll kick and scream and cry forever and ever, and me too."

That was exactly what he felt like doing. But of course, he was the adult, so he couldn't. He hung up the phone and put a daughter on each knee and tried to comfort them. Not that he was successful—and if Nessa did not return to them...

He left the girls' room. His confrontation with Nessa hadn't turned out the way he wanted it to, but at least they still stood a chance that they'd be back together again, for good.

Time. He was giving her time. But not time to let her think up hundreds of reasons why they couldn't be together. He needed to do something that would make her realize that they needed to be together.

Scott turned on the radio and relaxed in his recliner. He thought about Nessa and the emerald earrings he'd given her on Valentine's Day. She was the music in his life, perhaps music would bring her back into his life. When the DJ came on the air his scattered thoughts formed a solid idea. If the timing was right, he could do it. And by the end of next week Nessa would come back to him herself. But he'd need a little help from Monica.

CHAPTER TWENTY-SEVEN

Monday morning came too quickly. Vanessa dragged herself out of bed, got dressed, and was on her way out the door when the phone rang. It was Monica.

"Ness," she asked without preamble. "Where have you been hiding yourself? Mom and Dad were expecting you and Scott to come or call, or something."

"I know, I know, Monica, but I can't talk now, I need to be at work early today." That wasn't exactly true, but she didn't want to have any long conversations with Monica yet.

"Okay, I understand. I just called to tell you to turn on your radio and listen to 107 on the way to work."

"Okay, bye!"

"Ness!" Monica shouted.

"What?" Vanessa yelled, impatiently dreading to answer anything else she might feel the need to ask.

"Promise me that as soon as you get in the car you'll make sure the radio is on 107."

"I will, I solemnly swear, okay?" She'd promise anything to get off the phone and avoid any probing questions from her big sister. A coward, that's what she was.

"Okay, thank you very much." Monica hung up the phone, stopping herself from giving Ness the third degree. She hoped Scott's plan worked. She'd played her part. The rest was up to them. She prayed Vanessa would use some common sense, because she acted as if she'd lost it all.

Vanessa got into the car and did as she was asked, no, ordered to do. What was all this about anyway?

Vanessa had a twenty-minute ride to work and listened to this radio station anyway. It was a good mix of oldies and current songs, some soft rock, and none of that rap music that made her crazy.

Stopping at a red light Vanessa turned up the volume. She heard the DJ come on the air. "I have a sad, sad story about a man who's lost the love of his life. But he's trying to win her back. We don't normally do this kind of thing in the morning, but listenin' to his story 'bout broke my heart. So we're gonna let him talk to his girl over the radio waves. Who knows, maybe she'll come back to him. Listen to him, Vanessa."

Vanessa's heart skipped a beat. He couldn't mean her. As usual, whenever she was nervous her palms began to sweat. They slipped off the steering wheel. No way, there are lots of Vanessas in the world. This one wasn't her. The light turned green, but she froze as she heard Scott's voice on the radio. He did mean her!

"Nessa, I hope you're listening. I understand how you feel. And I know you're worried, but don't be...we could do anything together. I love you. Remember this song?"

The continuous blast of several horns caused Vanessa to automatically take her foot off the brake. She drove on to the sound of the music. Listening to the beat and hearing the words to the song got under her skin. Her body moved to the rhythm as the song described rivers, valleys, and mountains. It was a love song with a rousing beat describing a love that could overcome any obstacle. Vanessa knew Scott had chosen it for that reason.

As the soulful tune ended, the DJ's voice followed. "He's waiting for you, Vanessa, give him a call."

If she thought she was confused before, she was completely puzzled, and time was passing. The song made her feel a little more sure of herself, a little more sure of them together as a couple.

On the second day the DJ laid it on thick, and even started asking callers to phone in and plead with Vanessa to give her guy a second chance. Then Scott came on the air and simply said, "Nessa, stop."

The third song reminded her of how well they got along. All day long, the refrain from the song played in her head. Scott was giving her time, just like he promised, but he was making sure that time was spent thinking about him and the possibility for them to have a life together. The songs he chose insisted that it was possible. But still, she wasn't sure.

Vanessa woke up the next morning and decided not to turn on the radio. She was restless, indecisive. If she didn't listen, then she wouldn't feel so confused. That was an easy decision. With that settled, she got ready for work.

She kept her resolve for about thirty seconds. She had to hear his voice. A song was ending and the DJ came on. "Those of you who've been listenin' know the story about Vanessa and her mystery man who's trying to win her back. Vanessa I hope you're listenin' because this morning I got calls from some other ladies saying they'll take him if you don't want him. Take Slammin' Sam's advice and come on back before it's too late. But let's hear what the mystery man has to say 'bout that."

Scott came on the air. "I'm not a mystery man, Sam. My name's Scott, and I'd have to say sorry to those other ladies, Nessa's the only one for me. This song is special. It means a lot—to both of us. It tells how much I want you and only you. Nothing can change that, Nessa. Remember: heart, soul, music."

Her parents' song came through the speakers loud and clear. It was also special to them—another pleasure. She remembered hearing that song on the radio on one of their drives to the lake. They'd talked about her parents and how long they'd been married—thirty-eight years. She'd told him about this song, and how she'd hoped that they'd be together for that long. They'd promised to love each other with the same intensity. Then he sang that song to her on the levee under the stars, in that deep, deep voice of his. Vanessa remembered, and listened as the ache in her heart grew.

Scott was getting worried when the song was nearly over and Nessa had not passed the intersection yet. Did she hear the song? Was she even going to work today? Did she take another route? Did she miss the turn? He hoped not. Scott knew this song would pull at her heart.

Turning the van around, he drove along the bayou until he spotted her. She'd parked on the grass facing the water. He drove past, twice. Her head was on the steering wheel. Was she crying? He ached to comfort her, she looked so dejected. She was as miserable as he. He wanted to reassure her, to tell her that everything was going to be okay, that he loved her, and that everything would be fine, but not today. Tomorrow would be the day. Then Vanessa would come to him.

CHAPTER TWENTY-EIGHT

After work Vanessa walked into her apartment. Her phone was ringing. She quickly put down the bags she was carrying and grabbed the phone.

It was her mom. The last person she wanted to talk to. She'd rather have to deal with Monica. "Ma!"

"Yes, it's me. I've been trying to catch up with you for days. Where have you been hiding yourself, Vanessa?"

Vanessa? It was worse than she thought. "Nowhere, Ma. I've just been...sort of...busy," she answered, at the moment hating how close her family was.

"Too busy to come by the last few Sundays? That I can understand, Vanessa. But too busy to get fitted for your own wedding gown!"

"Oh no! I missed the appointment last week!" she groaned, just now remembering that she should have canceled the appointment, the dress, everything by now.

"And you didn't call to explain why I happened to be waiting at the Bridal Shoppe all alone on a Saturday afternoon."

"I'm sorry, Mama."

"And you should be," Joyce told her.

Vanessa wasn't dealing with the understanding mother. This was the other side. Here was the rough, tough dictator who was a stickler for responsible behavior.

"Okay, I messed up. I'm the worst daughter in the world."

"Not that bad," Joyce admitted. "I figure that you were preoccupied with Scott and forgot about the fitting."

"Oh yeah," Vanessa whispered into the phone. She was preoccupied with Scott, all right.

"It's understandable," her mom continued. "But Vanessa, you're going to need a dress to get married in. You are still getting married?"

But she wasn't getting married, or maybe she was. Whatever the case she answered, "I know," just to satisfy her mother. "Is there something else you wanted?"

"No, I was only calling to remind you about the dress."

"Okay, thanks."

"You will remember to make another appointment," her mom suggested in a tone that left no room for argument. That was not a suggestion. It was an order.

"Sure!" she answered. Vanessa dropped the phone back into its place and plopped onto the sofa.

She stayed on the sofa in the same spot she'd landed after her mother's call. She listlessly watched one sitcom after another until her stomach growled. She decided to cook the shrimp she'd bought from a truck vender yesterday. They were perfect for making barbecue shrimp.

She beheaded each shrimp, imagining one to be the big-mouthed line backer, then Daniel. The rest she imagined to be T.J. as she tore the heads off one at a time. She was getting vicious, but she was on a roll. Vanessa reached into the colander and found that she was out of shrimp. Too bad, she was enjoying herself.

She melted some butter in a shallow pan, added the shrimp and some seasoning, then put the pan in the oven. As she washed her hands, there was a knock at the door. Vanessa's heart skipped a beat wondering if it was Scott.

Looking through the peephole she released a sigh. It was her dad. She opened the door wider to let him in, and noticed his tool belt. "What's going on, Dad?" she asked, giving him a kiss.

"I just thought I'd come over and fix that broken window latch, baby girl," he answered.

"That's nice, Dad. But I would have gotten it fixed eventually."

"Well, eventually's not good enough," he sternly told her. "You'd think that no-good landlord or at least your fiancé would have fixed it by now," he told her pointedly.

"Uh—Scott's been kind of busy, and I just forgot to remind the landlord."

"Busy, huh?" Calvin said as he removed the potted plants. "These plants won't keep burglars out."

"But they'll give me a chance to run, hide or get help," she told him, putting a pot of water on the burner to cook some spaghetti to go with the shrimp.

He continued to work as Vanessa moved around the tiny kitchen. As she watched her dad, a comforting feeling surrounded her. Just having him here made her feel good.

Calvin grunted as he tightened the last screw. "What cha' cooking, baby girl? It smells delicious."

"Barbecue shrimp. Do you want to stay for dinner?"

"I've already eaten, but I can find room for a little bit more," he told her sniffing the air. "That shrimp smells too good to pass up."

He went into the bathroom. Vanessa heard the faucet running and her dad humming. He suddenly broke out with the chorus of his favorite song.

"Dad, why are you singing that song?" she asked, her eyes suddenly moist.

"Because I like it."

"I like it too."

"Then why do you look so sad, baby girl?"

"It's just that Scott..."

"Did Scott do something?"

"No, dad!" she interrupted, not wanting to shift the blame on Scott. She was the reason she was so miserable.

"Well then—," he waited expectantly.

Vanessa breathed in deeply, holding back the tears. She'd already cried enough. She'd cried all over Jessica and Adam, and she'd cried more than enough this morning.

"It's just me, Dad. I can't do it! I can't handle being married to Scott. You were right, it's going to be too hard to deal with our differences."

"You've lost me, that doesn't make sense, Ness. You told us you loved the man and he loves you. Vanessa," he asked, "what is going on?"

Always being able to talk to both her parents about anything, Vanessa gave in and told him everything. Every little detail that brought her to the conclusion that she wasn't strong enough to marry Scott.

"Not strong enough! You're short changing yourself."

"But dad, you don't understand..."

"I understand all right. I can remember a time when you stood up to a couple of bullies after school who were two years older than you to protect your little brothers."

"Dad, that was..."

"And what about the time you fell out of that tree and broke your arm. It was all twisted and bent, but you didn't shed a tear."

"Daddy, please stop, this is different."

"No, it's not. Strength comes from within. And you've got it. Remember that handicapped girl in high school. When everyone else was too scared to even look at her, you looked beyond that girl's differences and made a friend. Just the way you looked beyond Scott's."

"I guess I did. But this is different."

"I don't know how. Baby girl," he told her, forcing her to sit. "You know how I've felt about you and Scott to begin with."

She nodded silently.

"I'm not going to fill you with I told you so's. I don't have any because I don't see the problem."

"But Dad I told you…"

"Everything in life isn't easy, Ness. I've always wanted it easy for my kids. But life's not made that way. You told me yourself the two of you could handle anything. Well I'm telling you. Get up and handle it! You can do it!"

CHAPTER TWENTY-NINE

After her dad left, Vanessa went into the kitchen to clean up. It was there, as she scrubbed the dinner dishes, that fear began to subside and anger took its place. By the time she got through with the pan she'd cooked the barbecue shrimp in, she'd nearly scrubbed off the top layer of aluminum. This anger wasn't geared at anyone but herself.

Why was she running away from problems when she should tackle them head on? She had strength; she had courage; she had the guts to marry the man she chose.

She quickly changed into a denim dress and brown sandals, then went to her dresser. She pulled open the top drawer and uncovered her Cupids. Gently she lifted each one, reading the inscriptions she already knew by heart. Her heart, music and soul, the joys of her life, were all contained in one person. And she wasn't going to let her foolish insecurities stop her from seeing the truth in that.

Vanessa left her apartment with a definite purpose in mind. She would handle this before she went back to Scott. She wanted to rush on over to see him. But there was something she needed to do first.

She drove downtown toward the warehouse district, not far from the Port of Orleans, where ships from all over the world could be seen and heard traveling up and down the mighty Mississippi. She'd remembered T.J. bragging about living at the Cotton Mill, the newly renovated hundred-fifteen-year old building that was now an apartment complex.

She stopped directly in front of the lobby entrance. She sat and stared a few seconds. A security guard came to the glass door and glared at her suspiciously. She took her foot off the brake slowly, looking around for a parking space.

Vanessa had noticed the keypad at the front entrance. She suddenly remembered the braggart boasting about the coded access the Cotton Mill furnished to keep out unwanted people. She clearly remembered the look he flashed her way as he told his date about this little amenity. Vanessa hoped that he'd have at least one black neighbor, maybe two.

She parked, then walked around the building. There were several exit doors and a kind of supermarket/restaurant in the back. Vanessa peeked in as she passed and wondered if her best bet wouldn't be the front entrance and the security guard after all. But as luck would have it, the next moment T.J. emerged from an exit door only a few feet away. He was walking in the opposite direction and wasn't too steady on his feet.

"T.J.," she called, waiting for him to turn around and recognize her.

He stopped, turned his head, and squinted at her. "What do you want?"

"I want to talk to you." She did not move but waited for him to come to her.

"Excuse me?" He stumbled closer. "What do you..." His vacant expression changed to a sneer. "Well, if it isn't Vanessa!"

Vanessa stood her ground ready to block any move he made at her. She wasn't kidding when she told Scott she'd taken karate lessons. She knew how to defend herself. He was so drunk Vanessa didn't think he could hurt her if he tried. Still, she was on guard.

He stood staring at her, breathing heavily. Suddenly his nostrils flared, his face twisted.

Vanessa took the defensive stance she had learned years ago and practiced many times on her brother Randy.

T.J. charged full steam yelling, "You ruined my life! You…you…you black…!"

He never finished the sentence. Before he'd moved less than half a dozen steps in her direction T.J. had tripped over his own feet and landed flat on his stomach. He was still breathing; she could tell because he was making gasping sounds at her feet.

She thought how ironic it was that this same man, who believed he was so superior to her, was lying at her feet. Why had she allowed this man to fuel her feelings of inadequacies? Something she'd read a long time ago came to mind. "No one can make you feel inferior unless you give them permission." Vanessa couldn't remember who said it, but it was a great touch of wisdom and summed up her problems in a nutshell. She had let others make her feel that her choices were wrong and that she was too weak to rise to the task.

T.J. moved, rolling onto his side. Vanessa stared down at the pathetic man. As she reached out to help him up, she could smell the strong scent of alcohol surrounding him.

"Don't touch me!" Unsteadily getting to his feet, he glared at her. "What are you doing here?"

"Funny, I was just asking myself the same thing." She turned back to her Explorer realizing that she had nothing to say to T.J. But she had a great deal to say to Scott.

CHAPTER THIRTY

Scott woke up early Saturday morning. He was nervous. This would be the last morning to dedicate a song to Nessa. Laura came over to baby-sit for the entire day, and he had hopes of waylaying Nessa after today's song and spending the day with her. He just hoped he wouldn't spend the day trying to cope with her rejection of him instead of celebrating her coming back to him.

He wiped invisible dust spots off his newly personalized license plate. It was perfect. He kissed his daughters goodbye, hopped into the van, wiped his sweaty palms, and backed out of the driveway. This was it! He parked at his usual waiting place, called the station, and talked to Slammin' Sam.

"Man, the station manager loves you. You've been good for business. So many people've called to ask 'bout y'all, it's amazing. I think he's gonna start a regular thing with this dedication stuff. LOVE IN THE MORNIN', that's what we'll call it. It's like a soap opera. You got that week I promised you, man, so after today let us know what happens."

"Will do," Scott answered. Sam was a nice guy; he'd been rooting for him all week.

After he hung up he glanced at his watch. He was early. Vanessa wouldn't pass for another fifteen minutes at least. Thanks to Monica, he knew she'd be passing this way.

Nessa delivered baskets to the sick in the parish once a month. She should be finished soon and passing this way to head home.

He took off the watch to read the inscription again. It never failed to make him smile: Our love was a near collision. He agreed they couldn't miss each other; it was their time. But he'd never thought their love was on a collision course headed for disaster. Nessa not coming back to him would be a disaster.

He banished the thought. Hearing the DJ's voice announcing his name, Scott dialed the radio station.

"WLTZ 107 Slammin' Sam, here," the DJ announced.

"Hello." He cleared his throat. "This is Scott."

"Well, lover boy, do you have another dedication for Vanessa today?"

"Yes, I do. And this is the last one, Vanessa," he said speaking directly to her through the radio. "If you want me back for good, just follow the license plate. It shows how I feel, how I've always felt about you."

Hearing Scott say this was the last dedication only confirmed Vanessa's guess that this was her last chance. But he hadn't given up on her yet. Good, because her heart won the battle last night.

The soft strum of a guitar came through the speakers. She tapped her left foot to the soft beat that played on the radio. The artist sang.

"What!" thought Vanessa, as she listened to the first line of the song. It implied that he had given up on her. But as the song continued, she realized he hadn't. He was asking her to come back.

Driving along Bayou St. John, she kept her eyes peeled on every license plate. She stopped at a light. A maroon van turned in front of her. Its license plate read MYNESSA. That was it! That was Scott! That was their van!

Vanessa followed and blew her horn as he turned in the direction of the lake to let him know she was right behind him, following.

At the lake he parked, and she pulled in beside him. Vanessa ran over so fast that he didn't have time to get out of the van before she climbed in and sat next to him.

She stared again into those smoky-colored eyes filled with love for her. "Scott, I am so sorry. Please forgive me."

Vanessa handed him the note she'd written last night. "I'm back," she said softly. "And I can only plead temporary insanity."

He stared at the note for a long time, then looked at her. "I didn't like the last one I got like this."

"I know, but this one's better," she told him. "A pleasure."

He opened the folded page and read it aloud.

You're in my heart, my soul, you're the music in my life.
I can't live my life without music! Marry me!

In a flash, he laid his seat back and pulled her toward him. Scott held onto her as if he was afraid to let her go. "That goes without question. I thought you understood. I have every intention of marrying you. We should celebrate. How?"

She reached for the cell phone from the dashboard, dialed the radio station and said, "This is Vanessa. Play it again, Sam. And tell all those women out there that they're out of luck. I'm back!"

"Well hot damn, I think they're back together again…"

As the DJ jabbered on, Vanessa shifted in Scott's arms. She lay beside him sharing a seat meant for one, something she didn't mind at all. Facing him she studied his face. Scott had expressed his feelings through every song he had dedicated to her this past week.

She took a deep breath, sharing the same air with quiet intimacy, a simple pleasure. To be this close to him again was heaven. "I have to tell you again. I am so sorry," she said, punctuating each word with a kiss on his eyes, his nose, and finally his mouth.

Then Scott took over, crushing her to him, and devastating her with a kiss that showed the pain their separation caused. Breathing deeply, he held her head in his palms, caressed her smooth skin and declared, "Don't be sorry, just don't ever do this to me again. Don't let anyone or anything drive us apart. We can deal with anything together, okay?"

The conviction in those gray eyes told Vanessa that this was a promise carved in stone. "Okay, I won't be sorry. I'll have more faith and trust in you—in me—in us," she promised.

"That and your love is all I want, Nessa."

The DJ had finally stopped rambling and was playing the song again.

Scott asked, "Care to dance?"

"Yes," she simply answered.

Scott sang as they danced in the parking lot across from the lake, on a quiet Saturday morning—not under the stars, but in the bright sunshine at the start of a new day, prepared to share a life together. Despite any problems they might face, they would live and love—the greatest pleasure of all.

EPILOGUE

"A train! They're riding a train on their honeymoon?" Randy asked incredulously.

"You know that's something Ness would love," said Monica. "And it's obvious Scott knows it too. And not so loud, she doesn't know it yet. Scott plans on stopping at as many historical sites as they can along the east coast. He says he's taking her to Northern Territory, whatever that's supposed to mean. And you know how much Vanessa loves history."

"But on their honeymoon? There's barely enough space in one of those little compartments," Randy whispered. "How will they have any honeymoon fun?"

"They plan on spending the night at a hotel. They'll have lots of honeymoon fun then, I guess. And from the looks of them, I'm sure they'll find a way," Monica answered as Scott stole yet another kiss from his bride as friends and relatives wished them good luck.

The wedding was over! Everything had gone smoothly. And for Vanessa, it couldn't have been more perfect. Vicki, Megan, and Jasmine made beautiful flower girls, and Mark made a handsome ring bearer. Tony and Wendy's boys, Kyle and Brandon, had the honor of being junior ushers. Tony got a kick out of trying to boss around his uncles Josh and John who were the head ushers. Wendy, Jack, and the rest of Vanessa's brothers and sisters made up the bridal party. Even Daniel was there to wish them good luck.

Jack was the best man; Monica was the matron of honor. It was just perfect, her family, her friends, and her man. She felt very lucky and well loved.

Then it was time to toss the bouquet. Monica, looking stunned, caught it.

Vanessa laughed, took her husband's arm, and began guiding him to the door of the reception hall. "Can we go, now? I think I've waited long enough to make love to you. You've been holding out on me, and I demand satisfaction, now."

"That you shall have, Mrs. Halloway," he answered just as anxious, thinking about the satisfaction he was more than willing to give—the number of pleasures. There would be too many to count.

Following a fairly new tradition, the bridal party and what was left of the guests blew bubbles that surrounded the bride and groom as they left the reception.

An hour later at the hotel, dressed in the filmy white negligee Scott had given her for Easter and wearing the diamond heart-shaped earrings, Vanessa smiled to herself. Situations that had seemed so difficult were now resolved. Scott had confronted Travis Sr. and received an apology and a raise as incentive to stay, but eventually Scott would start his own business. Vicki and Megan had forgiven her, but took a lot of convincing and promising before they agreed to stay with Jack and Wendy for the next two weeks.

Vanessa figured that was her own fault. In time, they'd realize that she was there to stay, and would always come back.

Vanessa heard the key in the lock. It was Scott coming back with a bucket of ice. He took one look at her and smiled. "We won't need this, nobody has to cool off tonight!"

He reached for her nibbling on her upper lip, and caressing her back. "I see you're wearing my present. If you wait a minute, I'll slip on mine."

She couldn't believe he was going to put on those silly Looney Toon boxers she had bought for him last Easter, but when he came out of the bathroom one minute later he didn't look silly, he looked absolutely sexy. He wore those boxers and nothing else, except a knowing grin and a promise of satisfaction in his eyes. She hadn't realized it, but the boxers had a high cut that showed off his muscular thighs. The combination of those firm thighs, broad, hairy chest, and smoky gray eyes caused a fullness in her chest. This was her man, and she was finally going to claim him. And she did, beginning with his face. She caressed and nibbled every delicious part of him. Scott remained unmoving as Vanessa worked her way down to his chest. When she made her way to his stomach, she could feel his grip tighten on her shoulders.

Vanessa was surprised to find herself in this position. She inhaled deeply, loving the scent of him, feeling him shudder. She smiled and kissed his navel.

She was pleased with how bold she had become. Vanessa looked up at her husband, and his eyes urged her to continue.

She went on with her journey down Scott's body, nibbling on the waistband of his sexy boxers, and began to slowly pull them down with her teeth.

Scott, not knowing how he was resisting throwing her onto the bed behind him, was enjoying this sweet torture. His hand moved from her shoulder to those sensitive ears, which he caressed with gentle fingers.

Vanessa had to stop her exploration as a shudder ran down her spine at the feel of Scott's hands. She didn't think either of them could take much more. The boxers still rested low on his hips. Vanessa's hands moved down to his calves, up his muscled thighs, and under the silk boxers to the sexy behind that had first gotten her notice months ago. Finally reaching the elastic, she placed her palms under it, and gave him a final caress as she slid them slowly down.

That part of him she had yet to explore stood out straight and hard, waiting for her touch. The grip Scott had on her shoulders showed her how much he wanted her to explore. She gently, shyly touched him there.

Scott nearly exploded. "Enough is enough."

He did use the bed behind them. He pulled her back with him and rolled with her until she was under him, on her back, and at his mercy. He caressed and kissed every part of her, removing the gown as he went along.

And when they finally came together they experienced such profound pleasure that any thoughts or care either of them might have had of Vanessa's virginity vanished in the heat of the moment. Collapsing on the bed, and pulling her on top of him, Scott held her until their breathing slowed.

Finally calming down, he tucked her beside him and hugged her close to his side.

Seeming to be on the same track, they both said, "Thanks."

"What are you thanking me for?" Vanessa whispered. "Probably the same thing you're thanking me for."

Smiling, they faced each other.

"Pleasure number one-hundred-two," they said together. "We're explosive. It's fate," she whispered.

He traced her outer ear. "Yes, fate."

2007 Publication Schedule

January

Rooms of the Heart
Donna Hill
ISBN-13: 978-1-58571-219-9
ISBN-10: 1-58571-219-1
$6.99

A Dangerous Love
J. M. Jeffries
ISBN-13: 978-1-58571-217-5
ISBN-10: 1-58571-217-5
$6.99

February

Bound By Love
Beverly Clark
ISBN-13: 978-1-58571-232-8
ISBN-10: 1-58571-232-9
$6.99

A Love to Cherish
Beverly Clark
ISBN-13: 978-1-58571-233-5
ISBN-10: 1-58571-233-7
$6.99

March

Best of Friends
Natalie Dunbar
ISBN-13: 978-1-58571-220-5
ISBN-10: 1-58571-220-5
$6.99

Midnight Magic
Gwynne Forster
ISBN-13: 978-1-58571-225-0
ISBN-10: 1-58571-225-6
$6.99

April

Cherish the Flame
Beverly Clark
ISBN-13: 978-1-58571-221-2
ISBN-10: 1-58571-221-3
$6.99

Quiet Storm
Donna Hill
ISBN-13: 978-1-58571-226-7
ISBN-10: 1-58571-226-4
$6.99

May

Sweet Tomorrows
Kimberley White
ISBN-13: 978-1-58571-234-2
ISBN-10: 1-58571-234-5
$6.99

No Commitment Required
Seressia Glass
ISBN-13: 978-1-58571-222-9
ISBN-10: 1-58571-222-1
$6.99

June

A Dangerous Deception
J. M. Jeffries
ISBN-13: 978-1-58571-228-1
ISBN-10: 1-58571-228-0
$6.99

Illusions
Pamela Leigh Starr
ISBN-13: 978-1-58571-229-8
ISBN-10: 1-58571-229-9
$6.99

2007 Publication Schedule (continued)

July

Indiscretions
Donna Hill
ISBN-13: 978-1-58571-230-4
ISBN-10: 1-58571-230-2
$6.99

Whispers in the Night
Dorothy Elizabeth Love
ISBN-13: 978-1-58571-231-1
ISBN-10: 1-58571-231-1
$6.99

August

Bodyguard
Andrea Jackson
ISBN-13: 978-1-58571-235-9
ISBN-10: 1-58571-235-3
$6.99

Crossing Paths, Tempting Memories
Dorothy Elizabeth Love
ISBN-13: 978-1-58571-236-6
ISBN-10: 1-58571-236-1
$6.99

September

Fate
Pamela Leigh Starr
ISBN-13: 978-1-58571-258-8
ISBN-10: 1-58571-258-2
$6.99

Mae's Promise
Melody Walcott
ISBN-13: 978-1-58571-259-5
ISBN-10: 1-58571-259-0
$6.99

October

Magnolia Sunset
Giselle Carmichael
ISBN-13: 978-1-58571-260-1
ISBN-10: 1-58571-260-4
$6.99

Broken
Dar Tomlinson
ISBN-13: 978-1-58571-261-8
ISBN-10: 1-58571-261-2
$6.99

November

Truly Inseparable
Wanda Y. Thomas
ISBN-13: 978-1-58571-262-5
ISBN-10: 1-58571-262-0
$6.99

The Color Line
Lizzette G. Carter
ISBN-13: 978-1-58571-263-2
ISBN-10: 1-58571-263-9
$6.99

December

Love Always
Mildred Riley
ISBN-13: 978-1-58571-264-9
ISBN-10: 1-58571-264-7
$6.99

Pride and Joi
Gay Gunn
ISBN-13: 978-1-58571-265-6
ISBN-10: 1-58571-265-5
$6.99

Other Genesis Press, Inc. Titles

Other Genesis Press, Inc. Titles (continued)

Other Genesis Press, Inc. Titles (continued)

Falling	Natalie Dunbar	$9.95
Fate	Pamela Leigh Starr	$8.95
Finding Isabella	A.J. Garrotto	$8.95
Forbidden Quest	Dar Tomlinson	$10.95
Forever Love	Wanda Y. Thomas	$8.95
From the Ashes	Kathleen Suzanne	$8.95
	Jeanne Sumerix	
Gentle Yearning	Rochelle Alers	$10.95
Glory of Love	Sinclair LeBeau	$10.95
Go Gentle into that Good Night	Malcom Boyd	$12.95
Goldengroove	Mary Beth Craft	$16.95
Groove, Bang, and Jive	Steve Cannon	$8.99
Hand in Glove	Andrea Jackson	$9.95
Hard to Love	Kimberley White	$9.95
Hart & Soul	Angie Daniels	$8.95
Heartbeat	Stephanie Bedwell-Grime	$8.95
Hearts Remember	M. Loui Quezada	$8.95
Hidden Memories	Robin Allen	$10.95
Higher Ground	Leah Latimer	$19.95
Hitler, the War, and the Pope	Ronald Rychiak	$26.95
How to Write a Romance	Kathryn Falk	$18.95
I Married a Reclining Chair	Lisa M. Fuhs	$8.95
Indigo After Dark Vol. I	Nia Dixon/Angelique	$10.95
Indigo After Dark Vol. II	Dolores Bundy/	$10.95
	Cole Riley	
Indigo After Dark Vol. III	Montana Blue/	$10.95
	Coco Morena	
Indigo After Dark Vol. IV	Cassandra Colt/	$14.95
	Diana Richeaux	
Indigo After Dark Vol. V	Delilah Dawson	$14.95
Icie	Pamela Leigh Starr	$8.95
I'll Be Your Shelter	Giselle Carmichael	$8.95

Other Genesis Press, Inc. Titles (continued)

I'll Paint a Sun	A.J. Garrotto	$9.95
Illusions	Pamela Leigh Starr	$8.95
Indiscretions	Donna Hill	$8.95
Intentional Mistakes	Michele Sudler	$9.95
Interlude	Donna Hill	$8.95
Intimate Intentions	Angie Daniels	$8.95
Jolie's Surrender	Edwina Martin-Arnold	$8.95
Kiss or Keep	Debra Phillips	$8.95
Lace	Giselle Carmichael	$9.95
Last Train to Memphis	Elsa Cook	$12.95
Lasting Valor	Ken Olsen	$24.95
Let Us Prey	Hunter Lundy	$25.95
Life Is Never As It Seems	J.J. Michael	$12.95
Lighter Shade of Brown	Vicki Andrews	$8.95
Love Always	Mildred E. Riley	$10.95
Love Doesn't Come Easy	Charlyne Dickerson	$8.95
Love Unveiled	Gloria Greene	$10.95
Love's Deception	Charlene Berry	$10.95
Love's Destiny	M. Loui Quezada	$8.95
Mae's Promise	Melody Walcott	$8.95
Magnolia Sunset	Giselle Carmichael	$8.95
Matters of Life and Death	Lesego Malepe, Ph.D.	$15.95
Meant to Be	Jeanne Sumerix	$8.95
Midnight Clear	Leslie Esdaile	$10.95
(Anthology)	Gwynne Forster	
	Carmen Green	
	Monica Jackson	
Midnight Magic	Gwynne Forster	$8.95
Midnight Peril	Vicki Andrews	$10.95
Misconceptions	Pamela Leigh Starr	$9.95
Montgomery's Children	Richard Perry	$14.95
My Buffalo Soldier	Barbara B. K. Reeves	$8.95

Other Genesis Press, Inc. Titles (continued)

Other Genesis Press, Inc. Titles (continued)

Rocky Mountain Romance	Kathleen Suzanne	$8.95
Rooms of the Heart	Donna Hill	$8.95
Rough on Rats and Tough on Cats	Chris Parker	$12.95
Secret Library Vol. 1	Nina Sheridan	$18.95
Secret Library Vol. 2	Cassandra Colt	$8.95
Shades of Brown	Denise Becker	$8.95
Shades of Desire	Monica White	$8.95
Shadows in the Moonlight	Jeanne Sumerix	$8.95
Sin	Crystal Rhodes	$8.95
So Amazing	Sinclair LeBeau	$8.95
Somebody's Someone	Sinclair LeBeau	$8.95
Someone to Love	Alicia Wiggins	$8.95
Song in the Park	Martin Brant	$15.95
Soul Eyes	Wayne L. Wilson	$12.95
Soul to Soul	Donna Hill	$8.95
Southern Comfort	J.M. Jeffries	$8.95
Still the Storm	Sharon Robinson	$8.95
Still Waters Run Deep	Leslie Esdaile	$8.95
Stories to Excite You	Anna Forrest/Divine	$14.95
Subtle Secrets	Wanda Y. Thomas	$8.95
Suddenly You	Crystal Hubbard	$9.95
Sweet Repercussions	Kimberley White	$9.95
Sweet Tomorrows	Kimberly White	$8.95
Taken by You	Dorothy Elizabeth Love	$9.95
Tattooed Tears	T. T. Henderson	$8.95
The Color Line	Lizzette Grayson Carter	$9.95
The Color of Trouble	Dyanne Davis	$8.95
The Disappearance of Allison Jones	Kayla Perrin	$5.95
The Honey Dipper's Legacy	Pannell-Allen	$14.95
The Joker's Love Tune	Sidney Rickman	$15.95

Other Genesis Press, Inc. Titles (continued)

Order Form

Mail to: Genesis Press, Inc.
P.O. Box 101
Columbus, MS 39703

Name _____
Address _____
City/State _____ Zip _____
Telephone _____

Ship to (if different from above)
Name _____
Address _____
City/State _____ Zip _____
Telephone _____

Credit Card Information
Credit Card # _____ ☐ Visa ☐ Mastercard
Expiration Date (mm/yy) _____ ☐ AmEx ☐ Discover

Qty.	Author	Title	Price	Total

Use this order form, or call 1-888-INDIGO-1	Total for books _____

	Shipping and handling:
	  $5 first two books,
	  $1 each additional book _____

	Total S & H _____
	Total amount enclosed _____
	Mississippi residents add 7% sales tax